MW01166349

Gods Gone Wild

By

Dalton Diaz

and

Ashlyn Chase

ISBN# 978-0-692-24980-2

Cover art by Heather Newbury Almendarez, www.HeatherLynnPortraits.com

Warning: This book contains sexually explicit content which is only suitable for mature readers.

Great Zeus!

by
Dalton Diaz

.

Great Zeus!

Published by Dalton Diaz

Author's website is **www.DaltonDiaz.com**

DEDICATION

To Stud, who never turns into Zeus even though I can - on occasion – be as crazy as Hera.

SPECIAL ACKNOWLEDGMENT

Thanks to Ash, for always believing in me, and for sharing The Sherry and that crazy Yahoo group, ashlynsnewbestfriends. Join us!
http://groups.yahoo.com/group/ashlynsnewbestfriends/

My Beta Readers: V. Ettel, J. Chase & her cousin V. Burow, and authors Samantha Cayto and Samantha Wayland for their invaluable input.

Warning: This book contains sexually explicit content which is only suitable for mature readers.

.

PROLOGUE

"So good of you to show up, Epimetheus."

The ruler of Mount Olympus was not a happy camper.

Great Zeus! Why did I always listen to the...well, the Son of Zeus? It never ended well. To top it off, that asshat Dionysus was nowhere to be found.

When would I learn to think ahead like my twin, Prometheus? Yeah, remembering Pro's warning now wasn't going to help. Too little and too late.

Story of my life.

Okay, I loved Dionysus like a brother. Maybe that was the problem. Like my real brother, Dion loved to stir the pot and get me into trouble. And, like an idiot, I walked into it time and again. We're talking thousands of years here.

Our latest prank had somehow gone overboard, though I wasn't sure why. All we'd done was tease Pele until she blew her top and created a new Hawaiian island. Heck, that could happen by tapping her on the shoulder.

"You're a grown god!" Zeus bellowed, drawing my attention back to him. I winced as thunder rocked my ears. "I'm tired of cleaning up your mess just to have you screw up all over again. This time you will pay, and maybe you'll finally learn to think about consequences."

I stood up straighter. Punishment could mean anything with Zeus, depending on his irritation. Judging by the volume of thunder and lightning that punctuated each word, he was plenty pissed.

I wished I knew what I'd done that was so bad.

My confusion must have shown because Zeus's eyes narrowed and he leaned in closer to get right in my face. "Let me spell this out for you, since you don't seem to have the brainpower to get there on your own." The thunder and lightning stopped, but his tone remained as hard as Medusa's stone victims. "You two stooges teased Pele to see if you could get her to make a volcano erupt, even though you knew an eruption would create another Hawaiian Island. You with me so far?"

"Yes, Sire." What an asshole! Even Coalemus could follow that statement of facts, and I wasn't stupid. I just didn't tend to think things through before I did them. But I always felt bad if things didn't turn out well, and I actually cared about mankind, which was more than I could say for Zeus.

"You sat right next to Dionysus," Zeus continued, "in this very room, when I told my son about my plans with that fine young mortal woman who likes to wear wings with her undergarments."

"Yes, Sire." I nodded, figuring I'd better go along with it. "The one who models lingerie for that not-so-secret organization. You were going to disguise yourself as a rock star."

Zeus raised a thick white brow. We stood there and stared at each other until a trickle of sweat ran down my back. It was suddenly so hot in the room that I'd swear Hades was standing behind me, which wasn't entirely out of the question.

It didn't help when the thunder and lightning started up again right before Zeus bellowed over the noise. "Oh, for the love of me. Do you recall where this model and I were carrying out our plans?"

"Sure. Right off the island of Mau—" Oh, shit! "Great Zeus, we didn't intend—"

"Silence! Not only did you interrupt my plans at a most inopportune moment, Hera is asking questions."

It all fit into place with sickening clarity. After the fact. This time, I didn't need hindsight to kick my ass, though. Zeus was going to do it for me.

Something was still missing from the big picture. There wasn't any reason for Dionysus to try to thwart his father on purpose. There was certainly no love lost between Dion and his stepmother, Hera. Had he heard rumors as Hera must have, and left me to shoulder the punishment when he realized the magnitude of what we'd unwittingly done? That didn't sound like him. Trying to wriggle out of something by being his charming self, yes. Leaving his best bud to face Zeus's wrath alone? No.

But I wasn't about to ask Zeus where his son was. For all I knew, he'd been given to Hera for punishment, and I was lucky to be right where I stood. I shuddered at the thought. That was one vindictive goddess. I'd rather take my chances with Zeus, thanks. No matter how angry the ruler of

3

Mount Olympus was, I'd be more likely keep my head attached.

"Titan or not, I've always liked you, Epimetheus. Not like that jackass brother of yours." Zeus's tone was full of regret, and I reached for my neck, wondering if Hera would have been the better choice after all. "But I've had it. By the gods, you will learn how to think ahead this time. Go! Get out of my sight. When you awaken, you will be living your punishment. Have care, and you *may* come back."

Come back? I was hoping for more information, but Zeus ran me out with a thunderbolt aimed at my ass.

When you awaken…

I didn't go to bed that night. If I didn't close my eyes, I'd be fine. Maybe Hypnos could help. He'd successfully tricked Zeus before, so maybe he'd consider it a challenge to do it again…

CHAPTER 1

Bang! Bang! Bang! "Showtime, Keester! We have a situation brewing."

"Keester?" I rolled over and opened my eyes, and found myself in unfamiliar surroundings. The last thing I remembered was summoning Hypnos, and having him shake his head and place his hand on my shoulder. His touch had felt strange, like he was draining my energy.

It all came back to me with a jolt. This was it. This was my punishment.

Hmm, nice soft bed, and my surroundings looked like a high end hotel room. I didn't seem to be missing any limbs, no deformities…shit!

I jumped up and ran to a mirror before heaving a sigh of relief. The beard I'd grown to look older was gone, and my brown hair was now long and wavy, but I was looking at my light brown eyes, set in my face, atop my muscular body clad in boxer briefs. Hey, name a Titan, or even a half Titan, who didn't choose to be muscle-bound. If Zeus thought it added punishment for me to look like a prima-donna pretty boy, so be it. I could live with that.

The banging came again, rattling the door. "C'mon, Jack! Move it!"

Jack? Jack Keester? I rolled my eyes. Yes, Zeus, you think I'm a jackass. Got it.

"Give me five," I called out. Whatever waited for me on the other side of that door could wait a bit longer.

I used one of those minutes to throw on a pair of jeans that were flung over a chair, and continued to take stock of myself. There was no feeling of power coursing through me, I seriously had to piss, and my mouth tasted like I'd gnawed on Hermes' shoe after an Olympiad. I was apparently human for the duration, however long that might be.

It took another whole minute to don a shirt. Not because I couldn't choose one, but because no matter how many I pulled out, they were all the same. Every shirt in the drawer was black and stamped with the words Property of a Greek God.

Yeah, fucking hilarious.

The last three minutes were spent taking care of those mundane human needs in the attached bathroom. Then I took a deep breath and opened the door that separated me from Zeus's version of purgatory.

"You asshole!"

A plate went whizzing by my head and hit the far wall, splattering what looked like bits of bacon and egg in an impressive arc. Judging by the voice, there was a woman in the other bedroom. A very angry woman with an arm to rival the great Nike.

"I believed you!" the same voice cried.

Before I could enter the room, a blond guy ducked out, quickly followed by a flying slice of watermelon.

He turned to look at me with vivid blue eyes that held no emotion whatsoever, jerking his head toward the bedroom. "Take care of that, Keester. Now. This one has a temper."

I'd seen him somewhere before, but I couldn't place where. The guy stepped around me and into my room, and a second later I heard the snick of my lock.

I entered the war room in time to get nailed in the chest by a bread basket. There was a coffeepot and silverware on the room service cart. I eyed them warily, but the pretty little blonde didn't reach for either one when she saw me.

"Sorry," she said, sounding defeated. "I didn't know it was you." Then she sat on the edge of the mussed King-sized bed and started sobbing. "You were right. Tony Woods is a lying scumbag."

Shit. There were two things that got to me like no other. Crying women and hurt animals. The latter because, well, I had created animals. The first because it always reminded me of my sweet wife, Pandora.

After all this time, even thinking her name was painful.

I sat next to the crying woman on the bed and waited it out. Truth was, I couldn't "handle" the situation since I had no idea what had transpired— beyond the obvious. Plus, in god form or not, I was male. I had no idea what to say.

It was a solid ten minutes before she lifted her head to look at me, her big blue eyes full of tears.

Tony Woods.

I remembered where I'd seen the guy before. He was some young actor who thought he was the gods' gift to women. Oops. How many times had Dionysus and I cracked some inside joke linking Zeus's womanizing to the actor's actions on Earth? Somewhere along the line, Zeus must have caught wind of it.

The blonde took a deep breath and used it to steel herself. It was almost worse watching that coldness invade the soul of such a physically beautiful woman. "So," she said. "Did I rate the five thousand, or the ten thousand dollar payoff?"

Thankfully, since I had no idea what the Hades she was talking about, she pointed toward the low dresser where I could see a stack of papers held down by a pen. I went and looked them over until I had the gist of it.

"Neither. Twenty thousand."

"Yay, me." She crossed her arms over her chest in classic defense mode. "Of course, that probably includes severance, right? I can't imagine I'm his assistant anymore."

I nodded. "Would you really want to be?"

"No. Not unless you know of some way to poison him that won't lead back to me."

"Sorry." I partially lied. I knew roughly fifteen ways, twelve of them incredibly painful, but I couldn't pull off the anonymity part while human.

She brightened for a moment. "How about ways to make him impotent?"

I couldn't hold back a laugh. "Still sorry. You know, you don't have to sign this."

Her arms tightened around herself. "That would make me an even bigger fool. We both know sexual harassment complaints add to his desirability and make it easier for him to do what he does. Besides, I can't say I wasn't warned. The best I can do is hope karma is a bitch."

"Oh yeah." I nodded again. "That I can promise."

She gave me a smile that offered hope she'd be okay, then surprised me by flinging herself into my arms. I hadn't been thinking of her in a sexual way, but holy Hades, she was wearing some silky little number covered by an even silkier short robe, and it felt good to be held. Too good. The last thing this woman needed at the moment was a guy—

"I'm so glad you were here for me, Jack." Her voice was muffled against my chest. "I know it's selfish and totally un-PC, but I wish Tony was gay instead of you."

Er…no. Don't get me wrong; plenty of gods swung either or both ways, exactly like humans. Unlike humans, there was no judgment. I happened to be straight. Zeus could control a lot of things, but my sexual orientation wasn't one of them.

"Did I tell you I'm gay?" I took a chance asking. If it was planted in her memory that I had told her, it would seem strange if I didn't remember doing so.

"No, Tony—" She pulled away and looked up at me in horror. "Oh Jesus, you're not gay?"

I shook my head.

She turned beet red. In under a minute she had gotten up, signed the document, grabbed the check from the counter and yesterday's clothes off the floor, and was out the door. I didn't know what she thought she'd said to me in the past, but those comments must have been a doozy.

I sat where I was, going over what little information I had, hoping it would help me think ahead. Because I was trying. I really was.

My physical appearance was nearly the same, though my name was now Jack Keester. And wouldn't that be fun? I worked for an asshole actor who used women like Kleenex, one blow and thrown away.

Was I a bodyguard? Probably not. I had a feeling that job belonged to whomever had pounded on my door. Their voice had been much deeper than Tony's.

Whatever it was I did for the actor, he wanted people to think I was gay.

By the gods, there was a lot of thought that went into thinking ahead, and all I had to show for it was more questions and a headache.

The headache part walked into the room.

"I heard the door slam." Tony went straight to the dresser. "Yesss! You are so the man, Keester."

Good thing for him I was merely mortal with no way to summon my friends, or he'd look like a cockroach on the outside too. And my boot would be hovering. At least I could get one answer. "Why did you tell her I'm gay?"

"Aren't you? My bad." Tony shrugged, clearly not giving two shits either way. "Gotta say, it wasn't that hard to convince her, or to get into her pants. I thought she'd be more fun than that."

Yep. This guy was quite possibly the most self-absorbed asshole on earth.

"The studio is sending someone over to interview as my new assistant," he continued, gathering the papers. "I'll probably still be in make-up when she gets here. Make sure it's a hot woman. God knows what they'll send, since they seem to think I need some glorified babysitter 24/7."

And there it was. I was to spend my penance doing

damage control for this selfish bastard, and get cock-blocked along the way. Well played, Zeus. Well played.

When Tony left, the first thing I did was walk over to the window and open the curtain. I was clearly in a hotel on the Vegas Strip. Then I went over every nook and cranny of the place to see if I could find anything that told me more about my job.

All in all, it wasn't a bad gig if I could refrain from killing the human roach. Which was probably why I'd been made mortal for my time on earth. It sucked, but I'd survived worse. Much worse.

So when the knock finally came on the hotel suite door, I opened it thinking I knew what to expect. Female, about an eight rating on the fuckability meter. Human cockroaches had standards, and, Tony's misgivings aside, the studio loved publicity of his sort, including immorality. I was merely their insurance to make sure legal lines weren't crossed.

When I opened the door, what stood before me was a perfect ten by any standard, a twenty by mine.

It was Pandora. My dead wife.

"Pandy?" I breathed her name with reverence.

I'd never forgotten how stunningly beautiful she was, but it still hit me like a ton of bricks. That narrow, perfectly proportioned face. Those haunting dark brown eyes. The thick mane of soft black hair that hung halfway down her back. Abundant curves in all the right places.

Go ahead and call me a poet; she was perfection. It was also clear she had no fucking clue who I was.

She shook her head. "My name is Hope. I'm here for the job interview?"

Oh no. No, no, no!

"Hello?" Now she was eyeballing me like I had been touched by the Maniae, the spirits of insanity. "Is the job still available?"

"No!" I shouted. No way in Hades was my sweet Pandora getting anywhere near that—

"No, what?" the human cockroach asked as he approached the door. Damn, I was so rattled, I hadn't seen him or his hulking goon get off the elevator.

"Wow, you're Tony Woods," Pandora breathed with nearly the same reverence I'd used to say her name. "The studio sent me to interview as your assistant."

"You're so hired. This is Jack, my gay publicist, who for some reason is still blocking the door."

Fuck. Me.

I opened my mouth to set things straight, when my brain threw two blips. One, I couldn't let this happen. Two, if I protested, it would happen anyway. Without me.

Look at me, thinking ahead.

I stepped aside. I was trying. I really was.

But this was going to suck.

CHAPTER 2

First order of business, tell my wife I'm not gay. Second order of business, wipe that starstruck look off her face with a few hard truths.

Dammit, she used to look at me that way. Of course, I'd turned out to be an epic failure in the protection department. There's not much that's worse off than dead. I had to maintain control or I'd fail her again.

I ground my back teeth as I watched Tony's gaze follow Pan— Hope's ass to the couch. The brawn went off to the third bedroom in the suite, but not before he gave us a depraved look behind Hope's back that made me want to pound him into the ground too.

Tony sat with Hope on the couch, leaving me the chair. Surprise, surprise.

"That was Smith, my bodyguard," Tony told her. "He'll protect you too. There are a lot of crazy people out there, and I wouldn't want you to get hurt. By the way, please call me Tony."

13

The fake sincerity was back twofold, and I wanted to hurl. Couldn't she see it was the exact same look he'd sported through every nauseating chick flick he'd done? It was laughable, especially in full on dirt, scars and fake blood makeup for the action movie he was currently filming.

"I'm not supposed to be here, but I snuck away for a few," I heard him say. "I want to get off on the right foot before Jack fills you in on the rest. My last assistant left abruptly this morning. She got an offer she couldn't refuse, which isn't surprising. That's the name of the game in Tinsel Town."

I was seriously ready to vomit.

But Pan— Hope, dammit! was sucking it up like candy, completely enraptured. She always had wanted to see the best in everyone, and that curiosity of hers was a killer. Literally.

I was trying not to focus so much on Hope that I missed anything being said, but something odd was happening. The more the human cockroach spoke, the more her excitement seemed to wane. If I hadn't been watching so closely, I would have missed it, along with a flash of the birthmark below her right ear when she pushed her hair back. At that moment, the shock completely lifted and I knew, without a doubt, that this really was Pandora. She had always been good at everything because she was efficient, curious, kind, caring…and too smart not to see right through fake sincerity.

That's my girl.

Shit. Was. She was my girl.

Hope and Tony stood. The interview portion was over, not that she'd been asked any business questions.

"We're shooting one scene in the alley behind the hotel, so I shouldn't be more than a few hours." Tony said, before he turned his attention my way. "Make sure you fill her in on what she needs to know."

He called for Smith by a nickname, "Juice". At least, I assumed it was a nickname since the asshole came out carrying his sport coat, not a glass of OJ. Hope shot me a look of surprise.

What could I say? My guess was that he was called Juice for obvious reasons. Personally, I was going with the nickname The 'Roid. That fit either way you looked at the guy, since he seemed to be happily stuck to Tony's ass.

Huh. I'd have to remember that when I got back to Mount Olympus. One word to Dionysus would make it happen. If The 'Roid wanted to be a bubble on Tony's ass, so be it. All the more reason to find out where in Hades Dion had gone.

"So, you and Juice are an item?" Hope turned to me with a smile as soon as the door closed behind Roach and his 'Roid.

It took a few seconds for her words to sink in. "What? No!"

She held up her hands, cutting off more denial. "Sorry," she said. "I thought I heard you mutter what sounded like, 'I'm going to kill Zeus'." She pointed at my chest. "Property of a Greek God? When I heard Tony call him Juice, I put the wrong thing together. My mistake."

I nodded, hoping that would be the end of it and she wouldn't ask what I *had* muttered before.

"Shoot, way to get off on the wrong foot," she winced. "If you want to know the truth, I'd be more comfortable knowing Juice is gay too. I kind of like it that you are."

"What?" By the gods, I was starting to feel like a ping-pong ball in that bar in New Orleans that Dionysus favored.

"No offense." She sighed. "Look, as long as we're being honest, I'm surprised I'm even here. I was a live-in nanny for a movie director and his wife until yesterday, when she caught him in my room fondling my underwear. I thought she hated me even before that, but she recommended me for this job. It's…nice to know I don't have to worry about that from you. Not that you would, you know, fondle my underwear or anything…"

I couldn't help it. I burst out laughing as her voice trailed off.

"Oh my God," she cried, putting her head in her hands. "I can't believe I said that."

I couldn't, either. Especially since I had fondled her underwear. A number of times. Difference was, she'd still been wearing them.

Her words also made me remember that Tony's former assistant had trusted me. Right up until I'd told her I wasn't gay.

See me, thinking ahead again. Feel me, upgrading to a migraine. "I'm not with Juice," I managed through my tightly clenched jaw. "Never have been, and trust me, never will be. I wouldn't recommend being alone with him, but Tony is the one you have to watch out for."

She sat back down with a thud. "Damn. I knew something felt off. To be honest, he kind of creeped me out."

I nodded. "Like he was speaking lines from a movie, getting sincere in all the right places?"

"Yes, that's it! But that doesn't make sense. I mean, he's Tony Woods. He doesn't have to work so hard. He could have almost any woman he wants."

I sat on the couch next to her. "It's all about the chase for him. Give in and he's done."

She stared at me, probably wondering if I had told the truth, or if I was an even better actor than Tony. I waited it out.

At last, she nodded. "Thanks. I appreciate the warning. So, new BFF, what's a Pandy? Just curious."

I managed not to wince as an ice pick slammed into my forehead and twisted. "I'll bet you are, but I'm not answering that one. Be careful of that curiosity. It's a killer."

She nodded. "Sorry. I kind of hear that a lot. Um, are you okay?"

I nodded, albeit more slowly. A horrible thought had occurred to me. Did she have a human lover? A husband? Pandora had been a virgin on our wedding night, a bonus of having been created an adult. Gods, that had been the best night of my life. I wanted nothing more than to relive it then and there, but it would have to wait until later. "This job can be a relationship ender. You heard Tony describe the hours, and you'll travel a lot. Is there someone you need to warn?"

"No, not right now." She didn't elaborate, thank the gods. I'd heard all I needed to know.

The rest of the afternoon passed quickly enough. I showed her the discoveries I had made earlier, like the thick red notebook with the info she'd need, including daily notes from previous assistants.

It took her all of thirty seconds to realize there were missing pages, and that my initials were on each remaining page.

"Control issues much?" She shot me the same look of disbelief I'd felt at the discovery.

"Not by choice."

"Alrighty, then." She went back to reading.

The afternoon passed quickly, and, thankfully, the shoot ran over and Roach and his 'Roid didn't come back until late that night. I appreciated the time alone with Hope, but I was more than ready to hit the sack to sort things out in my head. I had a feeling I'd need to do that pretty often to pull off that thinking ahead stuff.

At last it was just me and my thoughts on the bed, staring at the ceiling.

As far as punishments went, Zeus had come up with a doozy. How was I going to keep my hands off of Pandy—er, Hope—let alone keep Tony's disgusting feelers off of her at the same time?

She did seem to believe me about her new boss, but so had the last girl. According to the log, she'd lasted a solid two months. Either I would implode, or Tony would be dead by then. Or both.

I also had no way of knowing how long my punishment would run. The thought of leaving Hope was unbearable, but if I woke up tomorrow back on Mount Olympus, at least I'd know she could be found.

But I wasn't going anywhere at the moment.

It was amazing how much it hurt that my own wife had no memory of our wedding night, or the heartbreakingly few nights thereafter she'd lain cradled in my arms. Centuries had passed and I still remembered every kiss, every caress, every sweet taste of her body.

Pandy's natural curiosity had more than made up for any lack of experience on her part. By the gods, it would have been enough to simply have her in my bed awaiting my touch, but she had returned every touch and taste in kind, not resting until she knew which ones drove me crazy.

Now that I was alone in bed, I let those floodgates spring open. I was instantly rock hard. Merciful Eros, I'd been that way off and on since opening the door of the suite to see her standing there. At last I could take care of the ache.

I slid my hand under the sheet and barely held back a groan as I wrapped my fist around my bare cock. Oh fuck, that felt good. It wouldn't take long at all.

I let my mind drift to my favorite memory, teaching Pandy how to please me with her mouth. She had clearly enjoyed kissing and licking her way up the insides of my thighs, her long silky hair caressing my legs. I'd had to work hard not to come before her tongue had finally run up my shaft, and then there was no holding back.

Her excitement for my pleasure and her pure awe of what my equipment could do had bordered on penis envy, until I'd flipped her over and showed her the multi-orgasmic benefit of being female.

I licked my lips, but had to settle for the memory of her sweet taste. It was enough. A couple more strokes and I'd be there. Yes…yes!

Motherfucking Hera Lover!

Pain like I'd never known shot from the tip of my cock to my balls, like they were being squeezed through an olive press. I let go of the shaft and curled up in a fetal position, praying I hadn't yelled aloud.

When I could breathe again, I gingerly poked my deflated cock. Nothing happened. What the Hades had gone wrong?

There was no logical answer, and I eventually fell asleep, still wondering.

"You cockblocked him."

I bolted upright to face my brother. "Prometheus, is that really you? What are you doing here?"

"You're not awake. I get one visit, in a dream, so listen up. You cockblocked Zeus, so he's cockblocking you. That pain you felt will hit you every time you get aroused. And Pandora's jar? First it translated to Pandora's box, and now humans think it means... Well, think about it."

"Wait. That fucking jar is now Pandy's—"

"Don't. Come." He spoke each word separately and succinctly. "Gotta go scrub my eyeballs now." And then my prick of a brother disappeared.

That's when I really did awaken, and much to my dismay, I was still in that hotel room from Hades. And I swore I could hear Zeus laughing.

CHAPTER 3

Two weeks passed, and I should have been enjoying myself despite the daily T-shirt gag. The harder Tony tried his usual tricks, the more Hope turned to me. If he hadn't viewed that as a challenge, no doubt my human ass would've been on the unemployment line.

Watching it all unfold was amusing, but the nights were killing me. Every time I closed my eyes, I dreamed of Hope. As Pandora, as Hope, it didn't matter. She was in that bed with me, touching me with those incredibly soft hands, trailing the liquid heat of her tongue over my skin. No matter how hard I tried, I couldn't make myself wake up before I hit Elysium…and epic pain.

It was the ultimate cockblock. After two weeks, I couldn't help cringing every time I got hard. And with Hope around, that was pretty damn often.

Right on cue, I braced myself as I heard the scrape of the keycard.

"The limo will be downstairs in ten minutes,"

Hope informed me as she tossed her room key next to mine on the desk. "Are you ready to go?"

I gestured toward my stuff by the door, hoping she wouldn't catch my wince. I still wasn't used to how incredible she looked in jeans, hugging those long legs and curved ass. I never thought I'd long for those shapeless tunics from the days of old. Come to think of it, access had been easier too.

Six hours in the back of a limo. This was gonna hurt.

Turned out Vegas was a post-production shoot, and Tony had simply extended the stay until we had to be on set in the Arizona desert for his next movie. Vegas was a kiddie playground to him, though he hadn't brought any women back to the hotel suite. Big clue that he planned to hit the gas on Hope when we got to Arizona.

For now, I had Hope all to myself for a six-hour limo ride. Roach and his 'Roid were catching a private jet later that night. Tony wouldn't say why we were splitting travel, but I was willing to bet it had to do with a majorly stacked redhead hovering in the background for the last few days.

He'd gone to "lunch", The 'Roid right on his ass, with a parting shot in front of Hope. The gist of it was that I'd get more personal time with Juice once we were on site. Great. I couldn't wait. The insinuation wasn't surprising, but a wink from the man in question was disturbing. That he showed any emotion whatsoever told me he was going to be paid well to make Hope believe he and I were in a relationship.

I didn't know if The 'Roid was gay, and I didn't care. I wouldn't touch him if I *were* gay and he sucked like a Dyson.

Hope seemed happy about our next location. Then again, she wasn't going to be spending nights stuffed in a trailer with The 'Roid .

It wasn't long before I slipped the bellboy a fifty and climbed into the limo after Hope. I took the seat farthest from her, but it was still too close. I didn't know if it was perfume, hair product, or her essence, but damn she smelled good.

"You know tips were taken care of," she pointed out. "You signed off on the log."

"Yup." I didn't expand on that. I couldn't. What was I going to say, "You weren't supposed to see that"? Or, "He'll always be mortal, so he needs it more than I do"?

"It was a nice thing to do." She smiled at me, and I hid my wince as my cock pushed against my zipper.

We hadn't even hit the road and I was already primed. This was promising to be as bad as Hades' place in summer.

The driver finished helping load our luggage, and we were off. He had raised the partition before pulling away from the hotel, but I double-checked the console to make sure the intercom was really off. If there was one thing I'd learned over the centuries, it was that any human could be bought for the right price. Come to think of it, most gods could be too.

"So," Hope said, stretching her long legs out in front of her. "Read any good books lately?"

"Just log books." I smiled at her. "You write a mean passage."

I was partially teasing. There had been nights when Tony had still been in the room and I'd had to bite my tongue to keep from laughing aloud. My favorite entry so far was right after I'd told her what I called the other guys:

There was a ginormous roach in Tony's bathroom today. I swear the thing looked like a hemorrhoid on steroids.

"We could talk about ancient Greek mythology," Hope suggested. "I've always found it fascinating, and I assume it's a passion of yours."

A passion? Oh, right. Today's T-shirt was white with an imprint of a fist holding a lightning bolt and WWZD in bold letters.

Well, that was one problem solved—instant deflation. I shrugged, shooting for nonchalance as I prepared to hear her fawn over the great ruler of Mount Olympus. "I'd hate to bore you with it."

"No worries, it's a long ride and I've been studying. I'll start with Zeus, the big kahuna." She sat forward, resting her elbows on her knees. "Don't you think he was kind of an asshole?"

I couldn't help it, I burst out laughing. I also decided to ignore the past tense reference. What humans didn't know, well, they were better off not knowing. "Definitely. But what drew you to that conclusion?"

"He was a womanizer, for one thing. Everything and everyone were his playthings, both god and human. I mean, he didn't seem to like humans very much, but he had no problem having sex with them. How self-serving is that?"

"Interesting." I sat back and crossed my arms. "Please, tell me more."

"Well, there's Zeus's wife, Hera. He screwed around on her, but I think he was afraid of her too."

"Another reasonable deduction. How about

Dionysus?"

"Playboy." She wrinkled her nose. "Or maybe party boy is a more apt description."

"Both," I agreed. "Prometheus?"

"Prometheus was okay for a god," she continued. "He seemed to like humans and to care how all worlds fared."

"He did, and he suffered for it." It was all I could do to keep that statement emotionless. "Did you know he had a twin brother?"

She nodded. "Shoot, I can't remember his name."

"Epimetheus."

"Yes, that's it!" Hope said. I could literally see the excited sparkle in her dark eyes as my name clicked with what she knew. She'd always loved to learn; it kind of went with the whole curiosity thing.

"What do you know about him?" I held back a smile even as my heartbeat tripled.

"Well, some stories allude to Epimetheus not being the brightest bulb, but he managed to create animals and he helped his brother do kind things. I think he simply wasn't much of a planner. Oh, and get this…everyone has heard of Pandora and Pandora's Box, right? But not everyone knows that Pandora was married to Epimetheus!"

"It was a jar, not a box," I automatically corrected, vaguely realizing I'd said anything.

"You do know your Greek mythology."

I didn't know whether to laugh, or cry. It was a surreal moment. I was posing as a mortal named Jack Ass, sitting across from my wife, who had no idea she was my wife, and who'd unwittingly just told me that I'd been married—to her.

It was enough to make anyone's head spin.

Bottom line, all that mattered was that she'd read between the lines and believed in me, exactly as she had all those centuries ago.

"You're amazing, you know that?" I couldn't resist saying it to her.

"Aww, I'll bet you say that to all the girls you're stuck with in a limo for six hours."

"Nope. You're definitely special," I assured her. What an understatement.

"Okaaay." Hope leaned forward again, her gaze intense with curiosity. "Does that give me the right to ask you a really personal question?"

It was apparently going to be a doozy, but what the Hades. "Hit me."

"Have you ever been with a woman?"

Oh fuck. I didn't expect that one, even though I should have. Deflection seemed the best option. "I'm with one right now…aren't I?"

Hope didn't bat an eye before looking down her shirt. "I think so. Unless I've been castrated and have a spectacular pair of moobs."

"Moobs?"

"Male boobs." She raised a brow. "I guess when you look like you do, the men in your life all look like Greek gods."

I smiled. "You have no idea."

And then Hope, being Pandora reincarnate, dug right back in. "So have you ever had sex with a woman?"

Damn that rampant curiosity. One thing I wouldn't do was outright lie to her, and dammit, Tony's whopper had gone on long enough. "Yes. Have you?"

It was her turn to smile. "All the time."

It took a second to sink in that she was talking about mastur—

A memory flashed in front of me. Pandora, laid out on our bed, legs slightly spread as she explored herself for the first time, at my urging.

Shit! We hadn't even left the city limits, and I was fighting thoughts that would leave me doubled over in pain.

Before I could stop her, Hope was next to me on the seat, her palm burning right through my shirt as she rubbed circles on my back. It was anything but soothing.

"I'm fine," I managed to grunt. "Get back in your corner."

The hand lifted, but she stayed right next to me. Did I mention how good she smelled? Shit!

"Do you need Joe to pull over?" she asked, her tone full of concern. "You wince a lot. Have you ever considered that you might be lactose intolerant?"

That did it. There were only so many indignities a powerless god could take. I looked her right in the eye and let every bit of desire show. "Touch me again, and I'll show you *exactly* where it hurts."

She stared at me in shock, then her eyes grew wide and she visibly swallowed. "Y-You're not gay, are you." It wasn't a question.

I answered it anyway. "Nope."

"So when I changed my shirt in front of you last week…?"

"I really enjoyed it."

"You jerk!"

I braced myself for the screaming tirade, the smack across the face, whatever she felt she needed to do. Regardless of the why of it, I deserved her anger and disappointment.

I wasn't ready for her to fist my hair and pull me forward to plant one on me.

By the gods, my Pandy was in my arms again. I heard a groan from a distance, though it barely registered that it had come from me. She tasted so sweet, felt so incredibly soft, smelled so damn good. It was all so right.

I deepened the kiss, my tongue searching past her sweet lips, coaxing her to open her mouth for me. We both gasped as our tongues touched and I was instantly lost again, diving in over and over.

It wasn't until she jerked against me that I realized I had laid her across the limo seat and stretched over her. My hand was up her shirt, the curve of her firm breast fitting perfectly into my palm through the lace of her bra.

It wasn't enough. Not even close. I could make love to her every hour for the next thousand years, and after feeling what it was like to lose her, it wouldn't be enough.

I wouldn't survive that again.

Don't. Come. Prometheus's warning shot through my brain, and with it came the realization that I was beyond aroused, yet felt no pain.

I slowly withdrew my hand from under her shirt and sat up, but I couldn't resist clasping her hand instead. I had to touch her, but I knew better than to look at her. Seeing her flushed with arousal, her lips swollen from my mouth would have me back on her like the jackass my current name implied.

I had no idea what might happen if Pand—er, Hope even came close to orgasm. Would the pain hit then? Would she end up in agony too?

I couldn't take that chance. I was trying to think ahead here. I really was.

CHAPTER 4

Hope fell asleep soon after our encounter. I wished I could say the same.

I hadn't been sure what to expect after my retreat, but once again Hope had surprised me. She'd stayed still for all of thirty seconds, then sat up and adjusted her clothing, all while leaving her hand in mine.

I hadn't dared to look at her until I'd heard a gentle snore, and gods, even watching her sleep made me want to be balls deep in two seconds flat. Pain flared up my spine, leaving me more confused than ever. Whatever, I was not letting go of *her* hand.

I wasn't sure what Zeus was trying to pull with this crap, but it was hardly equal to my accidental cockblocking. His conquest had been nothing more to him than a spread pair of spectacular legs.

Pandora had been my wife, and I had loved her deeply. Loved her still.

Prior to this, I had always thought Zeus liked me at least a little, and that he'd felt guilty for taking Pandy from me. Even as I'd grieved, part of me had understood that she'd been created to serve a purpose. That she was never meant to be mine forever. That no one, including Zeus, had expected us to fall in love.

What was happening now was beyond my understanding or forgiveness. And the worst part of it wasn't the cockblocking, or having Pandy not know who I was. It was finding out that Zeus could have brought my love back to me at any given time.

It made me wonder if I could trust anything as I knew it. Had Dionysus turned up yet? Did I have to question my friendship there too? I wanted to believe he wouldn't have stranded me if he'd had a choice, but what the fuck did I know? Apparently, a lot less than I'd thought.

I continued to study Hope as the scenery passed. She was so beautiful, so full of life even at rest. Pandora had embodied everything I'd loved. Hope was all that with sass, and I found myself somewhat in awe of the new side of her. Zeus couldn't mean to take her from me again. I wouldn't allow it.

A warning buzzed as the driver flipped on the intercom. I saw Hope's lashes flutter open.

"We'll be at the designated stop in Flagstaff in ten minutes," the driver announced. "I'll drop you off at the restaurant and wait for your call once I've refueled."

I reached over and hit our talk button long enough to acknowledge him.

"Sorry." Hope sat up and ran her fingers through her hair. "I didn't mean to fall asleep on you, but it was a long night getting last-minute stuff organized. Did you get any rest?"

"No."

"Any chance I dreamed that you're not gay, and we didn't really make out?"

"Uh, no."

She sighed. "I didn't think so, but I figured I'd check."

I bit back a laugh. "What would you have done if I'd said yes?"

"I didn't think that far ahead." She shrugged. "I guess my curiosity got the best of me."

I swore I heard thunder belting a comedic drumroll in the distance.

Definitely time to change the subject. "I wouldn't mind walking around Flagstaff for a bit after we eat," I suggested.

"We can do that. I just need to be on site a couple of hours before Tony arrives so I can fix any problems that pop up."

"Any chance of changing my accommodations while you're at it?" I figured it was worth a shot.

"Sorry, you're stuck with Juice as a roommate. Tony requested it, along with silk sheets, a cd player and a soundproof motor coach for himself."

"Only the best for the Roach Motel," I muttered as the limo rolled to a stop.

She was still laughing when the driver opened the door. I vowed to get her to laugh every night before I climbed into my predictably substandard trailer, shared with The 'Roid, no less. At least Hope would be sharing another trailer with the female lead's assistant. I wanted to believe there was safety in numbers, but knowing Tony, he'd see threesome potential.

I had managed to shake off all thoughts of Tony by the time we were seated at the restaurant. Hope and I didn't have much longer alone, and Earth be damned if I'd let that asshole ruin it. We had a great lunch, and an even better time exploring Flagstaff. When we couldn't put it off any longer, we climbed back into the limo for the rest of the trip to the middle of the desert.

This would be home for one to two weeks, depending on how filming went. I couldn't believe my eyes when we arrived. It was hot. It was dusty. It was also sunset, and the backdrop was one of the most beautiful places on earth I'd ever seen. The assorted cars, trucks, trailers and other equipment required to make a movie was a blight.

The limo bypassed the few fancy motorcoaches. Then the big line of travel trailers. We finally rolled to a stop in front of the first of three rows of compact campers still on trucks. It wasn't too far off from what I'd envisioned.

They were small. Very small.

I looked over at Hope in disbelief. "You're kidding, right? For two people?"

"It could be worse. They claim to fit three."

"Three what, children?"

She laughed, but I was serious. I was going to be stuck in that thing with Juice? His arm alone would fill half of it.

"I knew better than to tell you before we got here," she admitted.

"I'll bet. Isn't this a bit far for The 'Roid to be from Roach?"

"Yes. It's one of the reasons I needed to be here a couple of hours early. Our campers are supposed to be next to Tony's motorcoach. The request didn't go over well, so I knew I'd have a fight when I got here."

"Go get 'em." I nodded toward the door the driver had opened. I couldn't wait to see her in action. It would almost be worth sleeping like a sardine in a compact tin can with The 'Roid.

Thirty minutes later I was helping the driver unload the luggage into our campers, now parked on either side of Tony's super-deluxe motorcoach. I snagged the sleeping area that hung over the truck. Hey, I was there first.

"Do I want to know how you made that happen?" I asked Hope when we reconvened at the table in Tony's motorcoach to go over her checklist. Damn place was decked out better than our posh hotel suite in Vegas.

"I found the site lead and explained that simply moving two campers means Tony won't have to stay in a hotel in the nearest town, which happens to be over an hour away."

"Sounds reasonable," I agreed. "What are you leaving off?"

Hope smiled as she checked "Trailer Setup" off her list. "Or, he could leave things as they were and tell the director how his refusal to move two campers a couple hundred feet would cost the shoot two hours in travel time a day. His choice."

"Damn," I said with reverence. "Can you get us bigger accommodations?"

She laughed. "Nope. In fact, it wouldn't surprise me if he moved the two smallest campers in the worst condition. There's always collateral."

I nodded in agreement. I knew that one firsthand; I was sitting across from my biggest loss, hurtling full speed into the void again. It wasn't as though I'd ever stopped loving her, but I was a far cry from the open, festering wound I had been for an eon.

I must have winced, because Hope's brows shot to her hairline before giving me a look that could melt butter. "Well, well. We've established that you're not lactose intolerant. Does me being a bitch turn you on?"

Seriously? I would have laughed if my tongue weren't stuck to the roof of my mouth. "Your breathing turns me on," I admitted before I could stop myself.

The brief quirk of her lips was the only warning before she went in for the kill. "You're also not gay, and neither of us is seeing anyone. Remind me again why we're not acting on our attraction to each other?"

"We'd both get fired." And possibly fried to a crisp by Zeus. You know, that god you correctly think is an asshole?

"Ha!" Hope rolled her eyes. "We hate our jobs. Well, I like the job, but not the boss. I'll admit, I do need Tony as a future reference after my last job fiasco— Hey! That bitch didn't do me a favor by recommending me for this job!"

"About time that light dawned," I teased. "And for the record, I don't work for Tony. The studio pays my salary to keep his disease on an even keel."

"Oh crap." Her eyes widened. "Is he contagious?"

I shook my head. "Rampant case of Douchebag-itis. Worst one I've ever seen."

"Public relations?" She managed through her laughter. "You're in PR? I guess that fits, but you seem too… I don't know, honest for that."

"I'm not in PR. Believe me; he has an entire team on retainer for that. I'm paid by the studio as a glorified babysitter. It's my job to make sure he doesn't do anything that could deflate his box office draw *before* it happens. Like getting behind the wheel impaired, getting an underage girl drunk, or bedding a minor."

It was all I could do not to roll my eyes as realization dawned. I knew I was on damage control, but hadn't realized that my "job" literally meant I had to think ahead.

She was no longer laughing. "But over twenty-one is fine to impair, and over eighteen to bed?"

"I'll warn the girls, but I'm his babysitter, not theirs."

"That's lousy, but I suppose fair enough on your part," she conceded. "How did you end up in the limo with me?"

I hesitated, but she'd asked a direct question and I wasn't going to lie. "It wasn't me he wanted out of the way. It was you. His prey was clearly over twenty-one, and he wasn't driving, so there was no reason for me to babysit."

Understanding was swift. "Ewwwww! Okay, that's it. Change of subject, and I get to go first. Ready?" She looked me dead in the eye. "I don't agree that our attraction should take a backseat to our jobs."

Crap. I should have known she wasn't going to accept a half-assed excuse, or drop the subject. Problem was, I couldn't tell her the real reason without being committed to the local loony bin. Not that I wasn't already feeling like a resident.

The real reason involved not wanting to spend eternity rolling a rock up a hill, like Sisyphus. Or worse, watching Hope suffer in any way, or having her disappear again. I didn't know if that was thinking ahead or being paralyzed by fear. There didn't seem like much of a difference.

"I hated this job until you came along," I admitted, trying to tread carefully. "But if we have an affair and Tony finds out, he'll fire you and move on. If I'm lucky, he'll have me fired too."

I instantly knew I had fucked up. As I watched, that gleam came into her eye, the same one she'd gotten as Pandora when I'd told her not to open that damn jar.

She was intrigued, challenged, and, may the gods help me, she was curious.

"You have an incredibly sensuous mouth," she said.

"Hope…" I tried to say her name as a warning, but it came out strangled. It was hard to concentrate on anything with her looking at my mouth like it was the last bite of chocolate on earth.

"See, that's the thing. You haven't actually said no, and your actions scream yes." She stood and, before I could blink, she had straddled my legs on the bench seat. "Say no, and we're done here."

Yeah, right. Her beautiful breasts were at eye level, and I couldn't look away. Her nipples hardened under my gaze, becoming pronounced right through her bra and shirt.

"Touch me, Jack," she urged. "Like you did in the limo. I know you want to."

Oh, fuck yes I want to. *Desperately.* Just to feel her once more in my arms…by the gods, I was owed at least this!

I didn't have to lean forward very far to take one thick nipple, barriers and all, into my mouth. The sound of pleasure that came from her was something I knew I'd relive for eternity.

"Not enough," she gasped.

I released my treat, leaving a damp spot on her T-shirt. She whisked the garment over her head. Her bra was white and sheer, edged in delicate lace, the front clasp all that stood between my mouth and her skin. It had to go.

I groaned as her small, firm breasts with those thick, pink nipples spilled into my waiting palms. I was a breast aficionado through and through, and I had been obsessed with hers from the first time I saw them on our wedding night.

My mouth watered. If they looked the same, odds were they tasted the same too.

"Do it," Hope groaned.

I realized I was licking my lips, a mere inch from her left nipple. I wanted to look up, to see the expression that went along with that demand, but my eyes refused to obey. The sound that came from my throat when I engulfed that perfect nipple wasn't recognizable as a word, yet it spoke volumes.

Mine!

"Oh," Hope moaned. "Oh my God!"

Yes! Yes, I am! Energy surged through me that had nothing to do with actually being a god, and everything to do with knowing I was pleasuring her. I wrapped my arms around her and held tight, releasing one to latch on to the other.

I don't know how long this went on before I forced my gaze up. Hope was in pure ecstasy, eyes closed, head thrown back. I could feel her trying to move against me, but she couldn't break my hold.

Shit! Much more of this and she'd come anyway. Then what would happen?

It was the dash of cold water I needed. I made my

arms relax, intending to slowly back off. Hope had no such intention. Her nipple popped from my mouth as she slid down, moaning as she sank to my lap.

My cock throbbed and I bucked—in pleasure, not pain. There had been no pain this time. Great, but what the fuck did it mean?

"Shh." Hope put her finger to my lips.

She had stopped moving. I didn't know why until someone pounded on the door of the motorhome.

"The eagle has landed," called a female voice from outside, followed by footsteps fading away.

"Quick," Hope said, sliding off my lap and reaching for her clothes. "He flew into a local airstrip. We have about ten minutes if we're lucky."

The second the sensual haze started to clear, Zeus's bitch of a cockblocker shot up my spine and I gasped. Luckily, painful agony and sexual agony could sound the same. Sure as Hades didn't feel the same, though.

She had her clothes on and was out the door in under a minute. I tried to move, but even breathing was agonizing and I ended up curled up in a ball. Having the pain tolerance of a human truly sucked.

It took a few precious minutes that I wasn't sure I could spare, but it did finally ease enough that I could hobble out of Tony's posh digs and head for my shared piece-of-shit camper.

Hope was right. I'd never be able to tell her "no". There was one way around that; I couldn't let myself be alone with her. The thought was nearly as debilitating as the physical pain, which was apparently at random.

But hey, look at me, thinking ahead.

CHAPTER 5

It wasn't difficult to avoid being alone with Hope. Juice took care of it for me, which was the one reason I hadn't surgically removed the The 'Roid from my ass. He all but kissed me in greeting every time we were in public, and I was willing to bet he would have done that too, if offered more money. As long as he stuck to longing looks and almost touches, and it continued to serve my purpose, I couldn't have cared less.

That all changed about three days in, when Hope caught up to me walking to craft services for a quick bite.

"Rumor has it that you've got a problem, Jack," she said, trying to fall into step with me.

I sure did, and hearing her voice didn't help it any.

"Slow down," she demanded. "Geez, what's the hurry?"

Shit, no need to truly be an ass. I stopped walking and faced her. "Sorry, what's up?"

"Funny you should ask that," she grimaced. "What

does Juice do every night before bed?"

"Works out, I guess." I shrugged. I'd hit my bed, close the curtain, and put headphones on the second he came in for the night.

"What do you think it looks like from outside the trailer when he's jumping around and making those 'exercise' noises?"

The incredulous look on her face when I burst out laughing was priceless. "It doesn't bother you to be his bitch?" she asked.

I shrugged again. "It's not like it's true."

She gave me a long, uncomfortably assessing look. "Isn't it?"

Just like that, I wasn't laughing anymore. I had been so intent on getting through this punishment without physically hurting Hope that I hadn't given any thought to how it would feel to lose her respect.

I couldn't tell her that I was only letting Roach and his 'Roid play their games with me while I was mortal. I hadn't factored in that the ultimate trophy in their game was Hope herself, so by letting them get away with disrespecting me, I was disrespecting her. As an added bonus, by disrespecting her, I had managed to hurt her.

Hindsight. It was always fucking hindsight with me.

"I'll take care of it," I told her. "Tonight. And I'm sorry." I couldn't help myself; I reached out and stroked her cheek with my thumb. She was so beautiful, both inside and out, and she'd deserved better.

She sucked in an audible breath, and I dropped my hand and started walking again before I did anything stupid. Well, even stupider.

That night, when we all met in the luxury motorcoach to go over the schedule, I made sure The 'Roid had some business to go over with Tony before I said goodnight. Once I hit my own camper, I didn't waste time putting what little I had as a plan into place. I turned on the light I used to read at night and closed the privacy curtain of what I'd learned was called a cabover. Then I did the contortionist thing and slid out the side window before hunkering down out of sight with my back against a wheel.

All I had to do was wait with my own thoughts for company. It didn't take long before my mind drifted to the past. More specifically, to the memory of showing Pandora her new home after our wedding, one flat surface at a time. The jar had arrived not long after that, with Prometheus right on its heels to warn us not to open it. I could tell Pandy had a problem with heeding that advice, but I wasn't worried. I knew I'd be there to stop her if curiosity got the best of her.

It was a summons from Zeus that had finally torn me from her side. By then I'd forgotten about that damned jar, or I'd have buried it under the depths of Tartarus.

Of every coulda, shoulda, and woulda in my vast arsenal, that one topped my biggest regrets list. Hades, compared to that one, there wasn't anything else on the list.

Thinking of Tartarus made me think of Prometheus. It had been so good to see my brother again, even in a dream. If Zeus could bring Pandy back, maybe he could finally forgive Pro for giving humans fire…

Yeah, right. I didn't need special powers to know what the answer would be on that one.

I didn't realize how tense I was until I heard a door slam and footsteps, then Juice calling out, "Honey, I'm home!" The wheel jostled against my back as the camper took his weight.

It wasn't long after that I heard multiple footsteps approach. I peeked under the carriage and almost blew my cover when I saw how many cast and crew had gathered. Some were walking around, some simply standing there, but there was only one reason for any of them to be there at that moment.

One particular pair of boots caught my eye. A lot of the cast and crew wore Doc Martens, but one woman alone had purple ones with skulls.

And was that popcorn I smelled?

I thought it smelled good, but it didn't merit the moan of pleasure that suddenly filled the air.

Oh, right. The show had begun.

"Yeah, like that…higher…that's the way…"

Was he kidding?

The camper started rocking, a strained grunt thrown in every few seconds for good measure. I pictured myself in the overcab like every other night, rolling my eyes and turning up the volume on my iPod, thinking he was working out like a good little 'Roid trying to grow bigger.

Time to go. I hopped to my feet and came up behind the crowd. Sure enough, it was Hope filling those purple-skulled boots. She held a basket with a few individual bags of popcorn left. I grabbed one and dug in.

"What's going on?" I asked, all innocence as people began nudging each other and looking my way.

Hope, on the other hand, didn't seem at all

surprised to see me.

"Yeah, Juice likes that!"

I nearly blew popcorn out my nose as the sound of a palm repeatedly hitting bare skin rang out loud and clear.

"Anyone got room at their place tonight?" I asked the crowd. "Lysol? Preparation H?"

"Bug spray?" Hope added with a wink. "So if you're out here, who's in there with Juice?" she added, loud enough to be heard by all.

I could have kissed her. Best part was, I spoke the truth. "I don't know. When I left for a walk, he was with Tony."

Cellphones hit palms, cameras switching to video. I wondered who would win the tabloids payoff. This kind of info was usually passed under the table, but in Tony's case, no one was even trying to hide the sellout.

Juice gave off one last long groan and the camper stopped a-rockin'. The site lead, the same guy who'd given Hope so much trouble, gave her a thumbs up as he headed off with his phone still in hand. The rest of the crowd quickly dispersed, probably trying to find the best signal.

I was alone with Hope.

"So now what?" She looked at me after a moment of silence. "Do you waltz in the door?"

The question threw me. I hadn't thought that far ahead. "Why not? I'll wait a while, though. No telling what he was really doing in there."

"Eww. Let's walk a bit."

"Sure." I had some questions for her, and we'd be around other people.

Apparently, she had some questions for me too.

"What were you doing the other nights that you missed what was happening from inside the camper?"

"I heard the beginning," I admitted. "I figured he was working out, so I pumped up the volume to my headphones."

"Pumped up the volume?" She laughed. "On what, your Walkman?"

I didn't bother holding back a smile. People had no idea how deeply rooted some sayings were. That one was pretty new by my standards. "Outdated? Sorry. Believe me, it could be worse."

We walked in companionable silence until we came to the edge of camp. I could make out her features from the glow of lights, but it was pitch black about a foot beyond us. Beyond that lay the heavy vastness of the desert.

"There are a lot of beautiful and deadly things out there," Hope said

There certainly were, and without my normal connection to the animals, it was a great unknown.

"Aren't you worried how the studio will view gay rumors?" she asked.

Shit. No, because I hadn't thought about my human job. Now that I did think about it, I still wasn't worried. "Rumors aren't the problem. It's what a homophobe like Tony might do to dispel them that causes trouble. My turn," I changed the subject. "You set me up with a crowd. How did you know what I was going to do?" I asked.

"I didn't. Not for sure, anyway. I just figured you'd do something that would benefit from an audience." She reached out and tapped my temple. "You work from here."

She saw me. The real me. The worthy god I tried

to be even if I couldn't think ahead. I was doing better, and tonight was a good example of it, but it would have all been for shit if Hope hadn't brought the crowd. What I had done alone wouldn't have been enough.

I knew I should grab her wrist before her fingers tangled in my hair. Knew it was a bad idea to focus on that full mouth getting closer as those fingers pulled my head down.

But sweet goddess Ananke, I had to taste her right then and there or I would go mad.

She tasted like my sweet Pandora, with a hint of popcorn. It was a snack I'd be willing to dine on until I ceased to exist, which could well end up being soon if I didn't stop indulging.

I should have been able to pull back. There was no physical pressure to keep my head bent, just a slow, mind-blowing stroke of her thumbs to the back of my neck that shot sparks down my spine.

"Jack," she breathed.

I groaned and deepened the kiss, licking into her mouth for more.

I couldn't say when I pulled her out of sight behind a trailer and reached under her top to palm a breast, but that's exactly where we were, and that wasn't an orange in my hand.

"Jack," she tried again, turning her head when I growled in protest and tried to recapture her mouth. "There was a mix-up, and this row of trailers isn't being used."

I tried to focus on her words. The second I was lucid enough for them to make sense, I felt the beginnings of the pain I'd learned to fear. It was amazing how she both caused it and somehow made me unaware of it at the same time. As long as we were engaged in—

I sucked in a deep breath. What a fucking idiot I was! Zeus wasn't trying to punish Hope, he was punishing me. He was cockblocking me. As far as he was concerned, her pleasure had nothing to do with any of it.

Did he think it was a punishment to allow me to get aroused but not to come, as long as Hope was also aroused? He'd missed a crucial point. To me, her pleasure was everything.

I was ready to pick Hope up and rip the camper door from its hinges. I must have made some kind of noise indicating that, because she stopped me with a hand to my chest. She carefully peeked around the edge and I followed her lead with a stealth entry into the unlocked camper. Right. I didn't think word would get back to Tony, but gossip was a vicious, unpredictable bitch. We'd counted on it earlier.

Then there we were, facing each other in the dark. All of the campers were the same, so I knew the layout like the back of my hand. The cabover would consist of a stripped mattress with a set of folded sheets, ready to go.

I reached behind me and locked the door.

"Um, Jack?"

Oh, fuck NO! I didn't give a shit if she thought I was crazy, we were done with that name for the night. "Remember the conversation we had in the limo?" I reached for the shapely outline in front of me and found the bottom of her shirt, slowly pulling it over her head. "I really got off on that, and I want to fulfill a fantasy of mine. I want you to call me Epimetheus."

She didn't miss a beat. "Ooh, will you call me

47

Pandora?"

"Yes. By the gods, yes!" I claimed her mouth and wasted no time reaching for the front clasp of her bra, like before, but I couldn't get it to unsnap.

"This one hooks in the back," she gasped. "But Ja—er, Epimetheus, I don't have a condom. Do you?"

"No. Don't worry about it." I wrapped my arms around her and managed to undo her bra with minor fumbling. Worst invention since the chastity belt. Did humans ever learn from their mistakes?

"Whoa. Condoms aren't optional. I'm a safety girl."

"Can't get much safer than leaving my clothes on."

That actually worked in my favor, especially given how strong the urge was to get inside her as fast and as deep as possible. For the first time ever, I completely understood how Dionysus repeatedly got into trouble for wanting what he shouldn't have.

I heard Pandora's delicate gasp, but she didn't try to stop me as I tossed the bra to the ground and went to work on her jeans. When those were around her ankles, I yanked her panties down, picked her up, and slid her flat across the bare mattress of the cabover, leaving her feet to dangle over the edge. The minute it took to remove her boots and socks, then the clothes around her ankles, then my own shirt, felt like an entire decade.

"What's my name, Pandora?" I demanded, pulling her sweet ass even closer to the edge where I stood. By the gods, I needed to hear her say it.

"E-Epimetheus."

I spread those long, elegant legs and buried my face between them. I had a brief flash of the first time

I'd done this, shocking my virgin wife on our wedding night. She had come around quickly, but there was no need for any coaxing this time.

Soft thighs enveloped my head and muffled cries of pleasure made me wish I could see her face. I wrapped my arms around her hips and drew her up, licking over every inch of her sweet pussy before driving my tongue deep inside for more. Oh yeah, a feast for the gods like no other.

I was aware of my own arousal, but I had no problem keeping it in the background. I could have stayed there forever.

A change in the tenor of her cries brought me back to awareness. I couldn't say how much time passed or how many orgasms she'd had, but her entire body vibrated and jerked against my mouth, letting me know there was at least one more in her. I went straight for her clit with my tongue and circled her entrance with the tips of two fingers.

I heard her sharp intake of breath and pressed both fingers slowly into her pussy. Yes! She came apart, bucking and squeezing my fingers so hard I couldn't help thinking about how that would feel on my cock. The urge to come was nearly my undoing.

I somehow remained on my feet, standing between her spread legs, softly lapping at her pussy. There was no question that if I were up on the bed with her I'd be inside her.

Where it was too big a risk that my dick really would explode.

She released her breath on a deep groan. "Stop. Oh God! You have to stop."

I laid my head on her thigh, close enough to keep inhaling her scent while I could still taste her on my lips and tongue. I left my fingers right where they were, buried to the third knuckle. I wasn't ready to let go yet, and just in case…

"We need to find a condom, Jack. *Please.*"

Yeah, in case of that. The one way I'd been good at thinking ahead had been to anticipate her needs in bed. The safe route for us was to exhaust her.

Ironically, hearing that fucking name wrenched from her as she forgot our game helped me keep control. I took in her quivering belly, felt the shudders that racked her and squeezed my fingers every ten seconds, and I knew what I needed to do.

"Press your lips together." It was the only warning I gave, but it was enough to keep her from screaming. Or worse, saying the name I didn't want to hear.

My tongue had no problem homing in on her swollen clit with the first flick. Her body jerked against me like she'd been hit with a jolt of electricity, and the sound that came from her was a cry of pleasure smothered by her closed mouth. She was good to go.

Good didn't begin to describe it. Her pussy absorbed my groans as I began to thrust my fingers in a steady rhythm that built faster and faster with each pass. I had to slide my free arm under her to hold her in place as I let my tongue and fingers speak for me.

Those muffled cries grew louder and closer together. I caught movement and saw her flatten both palms against the camper roof. Within seconds, her entire body stiffened against me as she came in glorious spasms on my fingers, her clit pulsing against my tongue. I thrust hard before twisting and scissoring my digits to make it happen again and again until a long, low moan broke from her.

The sound abruptly cut off and her body went slack. The camper wasn't hooked up for running water, so I used my tongue to clean her up, ignoring her semiconscious groans of protest.

The second her body stopped twitching with pleasure, I was seized by pain so intense I nearly puked. At least I was expecting it this time, and, sure enough, it subsided with my erection. By the gods, I had figured out this part of Zeus's little game.

When I could breathe easy again, I rearranged Pandy's legs so they were on the bed, then hopped up there myself. I was going to sleep with my wife, dammit, even if it meant keeping my back to her. Besides, I wasn't going to leave her passed out alone, even if I could lock the door behind me.

Fucking Zeus. I knew I had to figure out the full punishment and get around it somehow. And if he took Pandora from me again…

No matter what, I couldn't let that happen. I had to think ahead, and I had to do it right.

CHAPTER 6

In hindsight—yeah, story of my life—it didn't surprise me to wake up alone the next morning. The surprise came two minutes later when Hope walked in with a true gift for the gods—coffee and a stack of donuts.

"Don't get used to room service," she warned, putting the stuff down on the table and busying herself with her cup. "This is an apology for passing out on you, even though it was entirely your fault."

I had no problem owning up to that one. I couldn't stop grinning as I swung my legs over and slid down, barely remembering I couldn't sit up first. I had enough headaches without adding a concussion to the mix.

When I turned around, Hope was holding out my shirt. She was such an amazing contradiction. Determined to address the morning after head-on, yet blushing between quick glances in my direction.

I took pity and put the shirt on. Thankfully, it was the same one as yesterday, a simple white T-shirt that read, "Where's a Greek God When You Need One?" It would have been harder than Hades to explain a different shirt appearing out of nowhere. "Hope?"

Sure enough, she looked directly at me. She also turned beet red.

"There's no need for an apology," I assured her. "If you are my bedtime snack every night for the rest of my life, I'll die happy."

I let the words sink in as I took a bite of a glazed donut, then casually licked the sugar from my lips before I downed some coffee. I wasn't kidding, and I wouldn't change my mind if we made it back to Mount Olympus where that timeframe was infinite.

She swallowed hard and sat at the table to join me for breakfast. After I thanked her for bringing it, we polished off the donuts and coffee in silence. I have to say, I was feeling pretty proud of myself. I had rocked her world and set the tone for the future. Not bad for holding mere human powers of persuasion.

We gathered up our trash and were headed out of the trailer before she finally spoke. "We should part ways here. Oh, and Epimethius?"

I nearly tripped over my own feet when she said my name.

"Next time, I'd enjoy having a bedtime snack too." She turned and walked away.

Don't think about it, don't think about it, don't think about — Ow!

I forced myself to walk back to my trailer, cursing Zeus with every painful step. Gods, to feel Pandora's soft lips close over my— Ow!

Relief came in the form of a distraction. Unfortunately, the form it took was the Human Roach standing in the open doorway to my trailer.

"Tell me why I shouldn't fire you too." Tony crossed his arms over his chest. Great. I had no choice but to stand in front of him at a severe height disadvantage.

"What are you talking about? Who'd you fire?" The question wasn't entirely a lie. His hissy fit could have been about any number of things.

His eyes narrowed. "My publicist woke me up this morning with some interesting news. Rumor has it you made a fool of Juice last night, and for some fucking reason it involved me and him getting it on. I pieced together his part and he took his last funded limo ride ten minutes ago. But you? You're nowhere to be found until you suddenly show up wearing the same ugly ass shirt as yesterday."

Out of the corner of my eye, I saw Hope slip into her trailer. She was out of Tony's line of vision, though it would make sense he'd checked for her there already. I was careful not to divert Tony's attention her way. She and her roommate were tight. As long as Hope came out wearing different clothes, there would be no reason to suspect her of anything other than getting up early.

"I don't know why you would fire me." I shrugged and gave Tony the same look of innocence that had worked on Zeus whenever I followed Dionysus down a hedonistic path. Well, it had worked until this last time, anyway. "I went for a walk before bed, and I forgot to grab my cell phone. When I came back to my trailer, there were a bunch of people standing around eating popcorn while they listened to Juice whip off a self-serve. I didn't want to go in there after that, so I crashed in one of the empty trailers."

His eyes narrowed, but at least he was thinking

about it. I was still patting myself on the back for coming up with something viable when I heard footsteps approach in a steady jog. Hope rounded the camper, wearing shorts and a T-shirt and dripping with what looked like sweat. I'd heard that some women could be ready in two minutes flat, but undressed, redressed, watered down and silently out a back window in that timeframe?

If I weren't already in love with her, that would have done the trick.

"Oh, hey guys," she called between gasps for breath. "Am I late? I thought we weren't meeting up until ten this morning."

She went straight into a cool-down routine. Tony did a double-take before he crossed over to his motorhome and went inside without another word. I thought it was funny until I realized how smoking hot Hope looked. My own words from the night before came back to haunt me.

Gay rumors aren't bad publicity. It's what Tony might do to dispel them that could be bad.

Shit. I called good morning to Hope for good measure, then headed into my trailer to shower and change. All in all, it had been a good twenty-four hours. I had excised a hemorrhoid, outsmarted a roach, and figured out a way to beat Zeus at his own game - by making my wife pass out from pleasure.

Things were looking up.

Ten minutes later, the three of us were seated at Tony's table going over the schedule.

"You do realize you're going to have to do double-duty as my bodyguard now," Tony informed me.

I almost blurted that I didn't have any experience. That wasn't entirely true, but I didn't think my brief stint with the Horae as a custodian of the gates of Mount Olympus counted. It had happened so long ago that I couldn't remember what Dionysus and I had done to warrant that particular punishment.

Hope gave me a swift kick under the table and I paused to think before I spoke. If I acted as Tony's bodyguard, I would always know what he was up to. More important, and most likely why my shin now ached, I would know what and whom he planned to do.

"No problem," I said. "I'm sure I have the right shirt for the job."

"Great." Tony rolled his eyes. The shirt waiting for me today was black with a picture of Zeus sitting on his dais, and white writing that read, "Real Men Worship Zeus."

It wasn't like I had a choice in attire, but it was worth it at that moment to see Hope try to hide a smile behind her hand. Besides, I wasn't a man. Well, I was, but it was temporary. Like Tony's days as a human instead of a real roach were temporary, because if he didn't get his fucking hand off Hope's arm…

"So," Hope moved her arm away from Tony's feeler and picked up her iPad. "You have to be in make-up and wardrobe in half an hour. I'll have your lunch sent to wardrobe, and I'll have the set buzz me when it's looking like you'll break for dinner. You're on the schedule for a couple of hours after dinner, too."

"Save your appetite for dinner with me." Tony turned the full force of his famous charm on her. "We have a few things to touch on."

"Sure." Hope made a few taps to her screen.

"Today's shoot is close enough to camp that they'll probably have you come back here to eat. I'll double check, though."

The feeler crept back up her arm. "I don't know what I'd do without you. You're amazing."

Dead. Fucking. Bug.

When Tony went into the private bedroom to get ready, I hadn't moved an inch. If I budged at all, it would be to squash him.

"Breathe, Jack," Hope murmured. "I'm surprised it's taken him this long to make his move."

She was right, but it didn't make me feel better. I took a deep breath and tried to release some tension when I exhaled. It didn't work.

"I can take care of myself," she assured me. "I appreciate the support, but don't do anything stupid, okay? I have a few tricks up my sleeve, and I need you."

Right. The bodyguard thing. "I'll do my best. Plenty of places to bury a body out here, though."

"Keep it together, Jack. Remember, I haven't had my midnight snack yet."

Oh shit. The tension was back, but it had nothing to do with anger and it was centered a lot lower than my shoulders. I couldn't let her do it, but fuck yes, I wanted it to happen. Desperately.

Then a thought hit me that sent me right into overdrive on the road to pain. I wondered if this kick-ass side of Hope would show up in bed. Her curiosity had ensured that nothing was off limits, and I had left her with no virgin territory within two weeks of our marriage. But she had always been the willing participant, never the aggressor. She hadn't been created with aggression or guile, and she hadn't been given time to develop them.

She'd had time now.

I could only nod as I went back to deep breathing. I was barely under control when Tony slithered out of his bedroom and we headed off to the makeup trailer. When we finally moved on to wardrobe, Tony's lunch was waiting, and there was a sandwich plate for me too. There had never been anything in the log about providing lunch for Juice, but it didn't matter. I was as invisible to Tony as anyone under the "crew" umbrella.

The difference on the other side of the trailer was astounding. The female lead, Virginia Ashley, greeted everyone by name and asked after their lives. Word had already spread about Juice, and it was obvious why I was standing there. They knew better than to openly show support, but there were quite a few covert encouraging looks thrown my way.

It wasn't until we were leaving that Virginia acknowledged Tony. Virginia Ashley had true star power, and if I remembered correctly, she'd recently married a cameraman she had met on the set of one of her blockbuster movies.

"Heard you had quite a night last night, Tony," she called out over the general chatter.

It got so quiet I swore I heard Tony's teeth grind before he answered. "Wasn't me. When you're ready to stop slumming it, look me up and I'll prove it to you, babe."

He slammed out of the trailer and headed for the waiting limo. I wasn't sure if I hoped he did or didn't hear the boom of laughter that was obviously at his expense.

"Move it, Keester," He called from inside the limo.

I took my sweet time. The ride would be short, but far from sweet.

"Fucking bitch." He barely waited for the driver to shut the door behind me. "They almost didn't get me to do this movie when I heard she'd signed on. She has the talent of a gnat and she's not all that attractive."

It was all I could do not to laugh in his face. Virginia Ashley had two Emmys and an Oscar, and her quite beautiful head was screwed on right.

"Why do you use women?" The question slipped from my brain to my tongue, bypassing any attempt at a road block.

He turned those laser blue eyes on me and, much to my surprise, the hardness he carefully hid from the general public melted away. "Do I? Damn, I'm more like my father than I thought. All that fake baseball and apple pie spin in my background is such a lie. I mean, who the fuck has normal parents, right? But mine were…let's say it's amazing I turned out as well as I did. I thought I was doing alright, but I guess I need to dig some more with my shrink."

He almost had me. I was a second from enthusiastically encouraging him when I realized what felt wrong. He looked vulnerable.

It was his trademark.

I stared him square in the face. "Freud would've had a field day with you."

"Bravo, Keester." He clapped, the vulnerable look gone in a flash. "There's hope for you yet. I use women because I can. The real question here is why don't you?"

I had. Before I'd met Pandora, I'd sown more oats than Quaker packaged in a year. In my defense, that number was half of what sat in Dionysus's breakfast bowl, and he could only claim half of Zeus's number.

Had any of those women hoped for more from us? Tony continued to rant about what a dickhead I was for not taking advantage of all the free T&A available. I disagreed. If Tony wanted to split hairs, he wasn't getting it for free. Those payoffs added up.

I'd seen his kind before, in both gods and humans. Visions of grandeur that occasionally came true. I could think of a number of humans, famous and infamous, with one ruler of Mount Olympus in particular who fit the bill. For all of their success and belief in themselves, they were born with a missing component that made it impossible to play well with others. They had no empathy. No feelings beyond for themselves and their own needs.

Ironically, humans tended to call it a god complex.

The moment of insight highlighted what a sanctimonious dick Zeus was for punishing me for ruining his fun with his model du jour. Even if the models he bedded weren't looking for anything more, it was no secret that someone did get hurt. Hera was Zeus's wife, and his philandering had literally made her go crazy.

The thought of repeatedly doing something that I knew would hurt Pandora was alien to me. I literally couldn't comprehend it. I was supposed to learn foresight, but when the fuck would Zeus get hindsight?

A strange warmth shot through me and Tony stopped talking about the merits of blondes vs brunettes and redheads to gape at me.

"What?" I asked in the silence that followed.

"Weird trick of the desert sun. For a second there,

it looked like you were glowing."

In a limo with tinted windows? Fucking idiot.

But I had felt something, and as far as I knew, humans didn't glow. I concentrated on bringing it back, but there wasn't so much as a flicker of warmth. There was plenty of heat to be found when we got to the site, though. It was brutal for the actors and crew who couldn't remain under the tarps, including Tony. If there were one decent thing to say about him, it was his dedication to his work. I actually thought I'd found something redeeming about the guy until I made the mistake of mentioning it during a break.

He looked at me like I'd told him it was hot out. "Well no shit, Keester. No effort, no stardom, no pussy."

Yeah, I wondered how that motto would work out for him in the roach world.

CHAPTER 7

I was really grateful for those tarps. I normally wouldn't worry about the sun, but had no doubt Zeus would think it funny to boil me like a lobster.

The heat also had its uses. By the time we returned to base for a dinner break, Tony was no good to anyone. His dinner with Hope was a cold sandwich, a cold drink, and a cold washcloth on the back of his neck. Hope and I sat with him in his air conditioned motorhome, where she managed to slip me a note saying we'd eat later. I wasn't sure what she had planned, but I knew what my dessert would be.

An hour later, we were sitting on a blanket behind our favorite empty trailer, sharing sandwiches and a gallon of iced tea. Tony hadn't been the only one down for the count, and the after-dinner filming had been canceled. Even so, we couldn't risk being seen going to my trailer.

"I've never seen a grown man so crazy about peanut butter and jelly," Hope said, taking a bite of her turkey club.

"I'm not crazy for it," I corrected her. "That's reserved for peanut butter and fluff."

"Marshmallow fluff? You have a sweet tooth!" She seemed delighted at the discovery.

I grinned at her. "Didn't I prove that already?"

It was my turn to be delighted as she blushed.

"I have a strange question for you," I said as I reached for another sandwich. "If you really could turn Tony into a bug, would it be a cockroach or an ant?"

I waited while she ate her sandwich and mulled it over. "Neither. I'd go with a male praying mantis."

I burst out laughing. It was brilliant. He'd have an uncontrollable urge to mate, but would never know if the female would bite his head off. "Perfect. Means I'll have to change his ringtone, though."

"Ooh, do tell!"

I did better. I pulled out my phone. She nearly doubled over with laughter when La Cucaracha began to play.

"Do I have a ringtone too?" she asked.

"Nah, just him. I figured he'll never call me if I'm standing right there, but anyone else is too risky. As long as we're confessing things, did you bribe the director to wipe Tony out today?"

"Nope." She took a slug of her tea. "I knew the weather and the schedule. It's my job to put two and two together and anticipate needs. But if I do need something from the director, I'll go through his assistant. He and I understand each other and our bosses pretty well."

That was perfect too. Her methods were the yin to my yang. We made so much sense as a couple, which left me more confused than ever. According to the punishment, I needed to learn how to think ahead. If I'd had that ability through Pandora all along, why had Zeus taken her from me in the first place?

Was Zeus actually admitting he'd made a mistake? That would be one for the record books. Or was he simply planning to make it hurt as much as he could before yanking her from me again?

If that were the case, she could disappear any second.

The thought made me study her, desperate to recharge those memory banks. By the gods, I'd always loved the way moonlight played on her skin, making it glow with beauty and vitality. Her long black hair was pulled back in a clip, and I couldn't resist releasing it to watch it cascade down her back. Before I could sit back, she captured my hand and laid her cheek to my palm.

The clip fell forgotten to the blanket. I couldn't breathe for fear of ruining the moment. The entire world, the entire universe, felt so comfortable and right.

"I know we met not too long ago, but I feel like I've known you forever." She sighed in pleasure. Her eyes were closed, but she didn't let go of my hand. "Do you…do you feel the same way?"

"Yes." Gods, I wanted to tell her the truth, but how?

"Have you ever felt like this before?" Her fingers tightened on mine. "So connected to a woman, I mean."

"Once before. With my wife."

I felt her emotional withdrawal, though she didn't let go of my hand. She was quiet for so long that I began to get worried. I was about to say something, anything, when I felt and heard her swallow hard.

"I don't think you would fool around with me if you're still married, and you're not wearing a ring. Am I wrong?"

"No. She died a long, long time ago."

She finally looked at me then, her brown eyes filled with sympathy. "I'm sorry. You must not have been married long, then."

She would figure I'm thirty or so, which wouldn't leave much time to be married and have lost my wife all that long ago. "No, I didn't get much time with her."

"Has the pain eased with time like they say it does?"

"Overall, I suppose so." At least, I had thought so. Until I had her in my arms and the thought of losing her again felt like Artemis had pierced my heart with an arrow.

"But you still miss her," she stated.

I nodded until I could manage a quick yes around the sizable lump in my throat. I should have known her curiosity wouldn't be satisfied.

"Do you think you'll ever love like that again?"

At last, an easy question. "I didn't used to think so. But now I have Hope."

She laughed.

I'd meant for her to, though it wasn't a joke. "I'm serious, but I don't mean to scare you. I can wait for you to catch up."

She nuzzled my hand against her cheek. "Catch up to what? We've known each other forever, remember?"

Relief flooded me. I leaned down to kiss her in the moonlight, a perfect kiss on a perfect desert night.

"Is this what you've been waiting for before we make love?" she asked.

And shit. I'd walked right into that one, and blown the perfect excuse to hold off sex. Mourning. Right. It was all I could do not to slap my forehead. Fucking hindsight. What good did it do if it always came too late?

I'm not sure if it was because I didn't answer right away, or the look on my face, but the good times kept coming.

"Jack, have you been with a woman since your wife died?"

I didn't know what to say. I'd sworn not to lie to her, yet the alternative was to sit there and tell my wife that I'd been unfaithful. Well, kind of. Despite the fact that she was in my arms now, she had been dead for more than a century before I'd finally listened to Dionysus.

I sighed, knowing I had to tell the truth, even if it came back to bite me later. Great. Wasn't that thinking ahead? Didn't do me a damn bit of good.

I chose my words carefully. "Some years after she died, a friend strongly suggested it would help to get back in the chariot."

"Chariot?" she laughed. "Isn't it supposed to be 'get back on the horse'?"

Oops. "His words, not mine."

"Did it help?"

"No," I admitted. "It got easier to do, but it never helped."

Even a few wild orgies with the Romans hadn't left me feeling satisfied. Physically wiped out, yes, but there had always been something missing. That special something that I felt simply sitting on a blanket again with Pandora.

"Are you afraid it's going to be disappointing with me too?" she asked in a hushed tone.

"No! Why would you think that?" Gods, the female mind was complicated. Male thoughts generally boiled down to three things, in any combo. I like it, I don't like it, and I have a dick. Guess which one I was thinking?

She stood and held out her hand. "Then let's go make love."

I couldn't say no. I didn't have to say no. I simply had to make sure I had control of myself and kept it.

I could taste her already. Thinking about the way she moved against me, the sounds of her pleasure as I stroked deep with my tongue made me hard enough to start that damn pain rolling through my balls. I needed to get more than one hand on her, fast.

She was faster.

I made the mistake of turning away to shoot the bolt once we were inside, and when I turned back, she was on her knees. My protest got lost in a strangled groan as her mouth closed over the base of my cock and balls, right through my clothes. I should have stopped her when the heated massage traveled up my length. Or when she pulled back and I felt her carefully lower the zipper of my shorts.

Knowing what I should do wasn't enough. I got as far as wrapping my fingers in her hair before she nuzzled into the open vee of my zipper, the only thing blocking the heat of her mouth a very thin pair of boxer briefs.

Then there wasn't any pain, just incredible heat inside and out. Gods, touching me like that had ramped up her arousal—

I felt the gentle scrape of her fingernails at the waistband of my underwear, and had enough presence of mind to know that if her mouth hit my bare skin, it was game over.

There was a reason I couldn't let that happen. What was—?

Prometheus had told me not to come. Game over could be permanent.

No!

She was licking and kissing my bare skin as she exposed it. Gods, one inch to the right was all it would take to feel that liquid heat wrapped around the aching head of my dick. I wrenched myself away so fast I caught her by surprise and she fell back to sit on the camper floor.

"Sorry," I said as I hit my knees in front of her. I didn't bother with her boots. I undid her shorts and yanked them down along with her panties. I had my tongue on her pussy and two fingers easing between her closed thighs before she could protest.

"Jack! That's not—"

I cut her off by zeroing in on her clit and sinking my fingers deep, and was instantly rewarded with her first orgasm. I lifted my head long enough to snarl my real name before bringing her there again, thrilled to hear her cry out the right name with pleasure.

I wanted more.

With her shorts at her knees, hampering her ability to spread her thighs, it took a bit to wriggle in a third finger. By the time I had all three in to the third knuckle, Hope was lost in continuous spasm, moaning with each exhale.

It no longer mattered that I needed to make her pass out again. I couldn't have pulled away in any event. Each moan was a gift on borrowed time, each pulse against my tongue the sweetest ambrosia.

When she did pass out, I pulled her into my arms and held her all night. Being that close kept the pain there, yes, but it also meant that if Zeus decided it was time, he'd literally have to pry her from my arms.

I awoke before Hope and took stock. My forearms were numb and my shoulders ached, but she was still with me. I cherished every additional second that passed before she began to stir.

"Hi." I smiled at her as soon as her eyes focused.

She looked confused for a few seconds. The next thing I knew, she was out of my arms, pulled up her shorts, and slammed out of the trailer.

Something told me it wasn't going to be a coffee and donuts morning after unless I got off my own ass to get them.

It didn't take a genius to know that Hope was pissed. I just wasn't sure why. She'd seemed pretty damn happy the night before, and I'd used the same method that had made her damn happy the night before that.

So now what? I sat on the trailer floor, alone, contemplating that for a bit. No ideas were forthcoming. It was just as well, since I'd fuck it up without her input, anyway. Hope and I needed each other, as Pandora and I had. I had the hindsight, she had the foresight. Together, we formed a whole.

It was a slow walk back to my trailer. It was early enough that few people were out and about, but there was no sign of Hope. The irony of that statement instantly grabbed me by the throat and was strangling me, right up until the moment I reached for that day's T-shirt.

It was a simple black and white rendering of Sisyphus, pushing the boulder up the hill. The caption read, "Never. Give. Up."

This message was not from Zeus. I didn't know who had snuck it in, or how they'd done it, but I was grateful. Truer words had never been spoken.

It didn't matter if there was no sign of Hope. She was still there.

CHAPTER 8

Another day, another grueling shoot in the hot Arizona desert. The only hint of cool came from Hope. I had tried to talk to her before Tony and I left. I got a frown and a reminder that the schedule for that day was wardrobe first.

I was on the verge of asking her, "What the fuck?" despite Tony being there with us when I felt her slide a note into my back pocket. If her silence was about Tony being in the same room, I could wait.

There wasn't a chance to read the note until Tony and I hit wardrobe. I was disappointed when all it said was 10 pm, and even more disappointed when the shoot ran over. Thankfully, after a security search of the motorhome when we got back, Tony said he didn't want to be disturbed by anyone.

No problem there.

I knew Hope would be alerted we'd run over and that there'd be no meeting with Tony, but she wasn't behind our trailer when I finally got there forty-five minutes late. I was both relieved and sweating bullets to find her sitting inside. I let my eyes adjust to the moonlight, then took a seat across from her at the little built-in table.

The atmosphere in the room spoke for itself. God or human, no guy liked these emotionally charged moments, and the first volley didn't help.

"You're living up to your name, you know," Hope informed me.

It took a few beats to realize she meant I was being a Jackass. It was the frosting on a long, hot day. One sentence, and I was pissed. "Nice to see you too. How was your day?"

She got up to leave.

"Shit." I caught her arm. "Look, tell me what I've done to make you angry. No games. Talk to me."

"Are you kidding me? You're the one who needs to stop playing games. If I wanted to play in bed, I could have slept with Tony and called it a day."

"And a job," I managed through clenched teeth. Thinking about them together in that context was a low blow that made Zeus's punishment feel like a pinch. "It doesn't matter how good you are, people don't hold value to him."

"At least I'd know where I stood. What's my value to you?"

You're my wife! I clamped my jaw shut against the shout that would have been heard across the universe. "Pandora—"

"Hope," she cut me off. "My name is Hope. No games, remember?"

"Hope," I dutifully repeated, not quite able to keep the edge from my tone. "Don't lump me in the same category as someone like Tony. You are beyond value to me, and I honestly don't know why you think I'm playing games."

"You don't want me to touch you."

"That's not true! I want—"

Quick as one of Zeus's lightning bolts, she'd straddled my lap, her tongue licking into my mouth as her hand dived into my shorts. I was rock hard with her first stroke, groaning with the second, and trying desperately to stop her by the third run.

It ended every bit as swiftly. Right on cue, when she left my lap to go back to her seat, a fucking boulder slammed into my balls.

"I'm curious" she said calmly. Too calmly. "You say that what's between us isn't a game. You say it's not too soon for you and that you're into me. So why don't you want me to touch you?"

Shit. I was feeling the physical pain from good old Zeus, and now the emotional pain from the land mine I'd detonated. What the fuck was I supposed to say?

"No games. Talk to me," she said, giving me back my own words.

"Pandora…"

"I'm Hope." She stood and went to the door.

Gods! This wasn't a game to me, but it certainly was to Zeus, and I was sick of it. I couldn't tell her everything, or much of anything, without the risk of disappearing. The one thing I could say was how I felt. "I don't want to lose you."

She hesitated at the door, waiting for me to start the explanation she needed. The truth, which I couldn't make sound sane, let alone prove.

My silence was deafening to us both.

"Funny, that's exactly what you just chose." She went out the door.

I'd gone back to my own trailer, fully expecting to

wake up to find myself on Mount Olympus, game over. In one way, I was ready. Even if Zeus blocked me from getting to Hope, I knew she existed. I'd find her and at least watch over her. There were a lot of guys like Tony in her world. Too many.

In hindsight—fuck me—I understood where she was coming from. She'd opened up to me and expected the same back, and I shut her down. I'd used a pleasing method, but a wall of pleasure was still a wall.

I'd taken a chance, and lost. Once again, my efforts at thinking ahead had created the very issue I was trying to avoid. Go figure.

We were done. It was with a heavy heart that I finally fell asleep close to dawn, popping awake in fear just a couple of hours later. I was still in my trailer. The scary part was I didn't know if it was because Zeus didn't think I had suffered enough, or because there was still a chance with Hope. I got my answer when I saw the T-shirt of the day. It was white, picturing a victorious Zeus, underneath which simply read, "Team Zeus."

"If you won your fucked-up game, why am I still here?" I asked the empty trailer.

I instantly regretted saying it aloud. Feeling somewhat resigned to going home was not the same as asking to go. If I had to leave Pandora, I would go down fighting.

I rolled the damn shirt up in a ball and threw it in the trash. Yeah, there would be another exactly like it in every drawer, but it felt good to let Zeus know what I thought of his grinning face. Going shirtless would have been better, but I was in the desert. Even I could think ahead enough to know that would be stupid.

Sure enough, there was a brand new, wrinkle-free version of the shirt available. I put it on and headed out for coffee. I wouldn't need the caffeine back on Mount Olympus, but I sure as Hades appreciated it now.

Hope was already in Tony's motorhome when I got there, brewing the asshole a cup of coffee with his personal pod machine. Gods forbid he pull a lever for himself on something so mundane, or, even worse, share.

I figured he was in his bedroom, because Hope and I were alone for the moment.

"Round two." I put my to-go cup offering on the counter.

She turned to face me with a genuine smile. "Thanks. Definitely a multi cup morning."

She looked tired, and I was most likely the cause. "Are you okay?"

"I'm a big girl, Jack. I'll be fine."

"You have to know that I do want you," I said, lowering my voice further, but I was damned well going to say it.

To my relief, she nodded. "All in all, it would have hurt worse had we slept together. It's not about that, though. You do understand that, right? I can't have a relationship with someone who can't be open and honest with me."

I wanted to be. Gods, I wanted to be. But you can't have a relationship with a crazy man, or a god who suddenly disappears, either. "I'll work on it."

"You do that." She nodded again. "And when you figure things out, look me up. You never know, we may both still be single."

May? That was when it dawned on me that watching over her meant watching her love life move on without me. Great. That I manage to think of ahead of time, to fester until it actually happened. Just the idea of it made my head start to hurt.

Oh what a tangled web we weave...

Fucking Shakespeare, always preaching. Never could stand the guy.

"Oh good, the gang's all here." Tony came out of the back bedroom, right on cue. "Great news, Keester. There was a reschedule, and I'm not shooting today. I think this beautiful lady here needs a break, right babe?" He took his coffee from Hope, letting his hand and gaze linger. "Let's take a drive out to Sedona. It's only a couple of hours."

"Sounds fun," Hope said, barely missing a beat.

Calling an employee babe? Seriously? "I'd like to hire extra security. I don't have the experience to keep you safe in a crowd," I pointed out. Like I gave a roach's ass about Tony's safety. I wanted witnesses, and someone else to play bodyguard so I could keep Hope safe from the scumbag already riding in the limo.

Headache from trying to think ahead or not, I had learned from the night The 'Roid got fired. I was feelin' proud until Hope took a step backward and stomped on my toes with the heel of her purple-skulled Doc Martens.

"Oh, sorry." She whirled around to face me. "Did I hurt you?"

With her back now to Tony, she put her finger to her lips.

It was too late.

"That's a great idea, Keester," Tony said. "In fact,

take the day off. We won't need you."

The fuck that was going to happen. But Hope's eyes now widened for emphasis as she once more tapped her finger to her lips. I held back a snarl and kept my mouth shut. Her foresight would be much more effective than me trying to explain to the police how Tony's head got crushed under a stationary motorhome.

"I'll need some time to take care of the security issue," Hope turned back toward Tony once she was sure I would be quiet.

Tony gave her one of his patented movie star smiles. "We can meet back here in one hour. I have a few things to take care of too. Keester, you heard the lady. Get lost."

I did leave, after a barely discernible nod from Hope, and I stayed outside the motorhome to catch her. It was a few minutes before Tony's driver went in and Hope came out. I followed her into her blessedly empty trailer without invitation.

"You're not going without me," I flatly stated the second the door closed behind us.

Hope stopped in her tracks a foot from me and turned, crossing her arms. "Excuse me?"

"You heard me."

"You're the one who got yourself booted out of the limo," she pointed out.

I felt the heat creep up my neck. "That was a mistake. I was trying to make it a group outing."

"I told you I can take care of myself. I'd be perfectly safe alone with him, and now there will be a group. You just won't be in it."

"Like Hades I won't be," I ground out. "I know you. I'll bet you have five different ways you can fix this."

She shrugged. "There's nothing to fix."

I didn't know if she intended it, but her words sounded sad, almost defeated. It suddenly wasn't about her being alone with Tony. Might never have been about it in the first place.

She was in my arms, plastered against the closed door to the bathroom, before I could form another thought. "There's everything to fix," I said, closing my mouth over hers.

I ground against her, out of control before I'd even touched her. I did hear one brief cry of protest, but it was gone as quickly as it came. She was kissing me back, moving what little bit she could to press me harder between her legs. There was no way she could mistake my desire for her.

I would have kept going. I wanted her stripped and on her back, open to me for a hard ride. She belonged to me every bit as much as I belonged to her. Anything else—Zeus, pain, Tony—could all be damned.

"Jack!"

It was her desperate tone that finally got through. At some point I had apparently pulled her away from the door and was trying to ease her to the floor. Right. The bed would be better. I didn't know if she or her roommate had claimed the cabover, and I didn't care. That was where we were going.

"Jack!"

I took a deep breath and tried to focus. She was clinging to me, stroking my hair, trying to calm me.

"You with me?" she asked softly.

I could only nod. Gods, she was so fucking beautiful. This part of the torture was over. If I were going to disappear at any moment, I was damned well going to make love to my wife before it happened.

Heat suffused me, and Hope stepped back as far as she could in the tiny trailer.

"Y-you're glowing!" she gasped.

Was it any wonder? I had to have the worst case of blue balls known to man.

"Is this part of what you couldn't tell me?" she whispered. Unfortunately, I wasn't sure if it was in fear, or awe.

I nodded, feeling the heat subside along with everything else. "Don't be afraid." I held out my now-normal-looking hand. "I won't hurt you. If nothing else, you know that."

She hesitated, but finally nodded and put her hand in mine.

"And know that I love you." I drew her in closer and gently kissed her. "I can't tell you more than that right now, but if you believe those two things, there's a chance this can work."

"This?" she whispered.

"Us. You and me together. This." I kissed her again and the rest of the world fell away. I wasn't sure what world we'd be in when we dropped back to reality, but it didn't matter. Hope was with me.

"Well, isn't this so much more special than my coming to ask you to dinner," Tony scoffed. Does his real boyfriend know?"

Neither Hope nor I jumped apart. It was more of a slow, reluctant drop back to the present. The present on earth, dammit. What had passed between us was far more powerful than an invasion by a human cockroach.

"Yes," Hope said, not bothering to hide her

irritation. "And I love him too."

I tightened my hand in hers. She'd stepped in it this time, worse than I had before. She'd just told Tony she was into threesomes.

This was one scenario where it wouldn't do her any good to think ahead if she couldn't think like a guy.

Sure enough, Tony grinned. "Wild woman! I love it. Guess that answers which one of you is getting fired. Pack your shit, Keester. Change of plans. We'll be using the limo, so we'll go to Flagstaff instead and dump you there." He turned and walked out, leaving the door open.

"I'm sorry." Hope sighed. "What will the studio say?"

"That he doesn't have the authority to fire me, or he'd have done it by now."

Unfortunately, I was wrong. Ten minutes later, I had fielded a phone call from the earthly powers that be. There was a plane ticket waiting for me in Flagstaff. To where, I had no clue. Planes didn't exactly fly to my Mount Olympus.

I also had a text from Hope telling me not to get on the plane. If she couldn't get Tony to change his mind, she'd be going with me. Sure enough, when it got close to the appointed hour, I heard a trunk close from behind my trailer. I looked out my back window, a spot not visible to Tony, in time to see Hope give the driver a hug. Not money, a hug. She was amazing.

Ten minutes after that, we were on our way to Flagstaff. I was surprised when Tony insisted I sit in back. The hired security firm was in Flagstaff, so I was the security, but I'd have qualms about having a guy I'd just fired guarding my ass.

It made more sense when he sat next to Hope and immediately started to point out why he would be a better prospect for her, including setting up a threesome where she would be the main focus. Unless she preferred it with another woman so they could focus on him, of course. Because what woman wouldn't want that?

I concentrated on trying to make his hair fall out, and Hope tried to get him to change his mind about firing me. As long as he didn't touch her, I could take it. After all, whether Tony decided to fire me at the end of the ride or not, Hope would be with me.

We were about ten miles out of Flagstaff when Tony leaned over and hit the intercom. "Pull over. I gotta go."

Right. This had to be another attempt to show Hope his "better prospect" in front of me. Her surreptitious eye roll said she thought same thing. I had heard rumors that he was well hung, but I had news for him: if a Titan could choose to be muscle bound…

"Today, Keester," Tony called back into the limo.

"I'm good," I assured him.

"I don't give a crap if you have to piss or not. You're no good to my safety in the limo."

"Not true," I muttered.

Hope was biting her lip trying not to laugh. "Don't worry. I promise I'll only look at yours."

It was all I could do not to kiss her as I left the limo.

The next thing I knew, Tony dived back in, barely shutting the door on Hope calling for me. The limo took off, and a couple of water bottles flew out of the driver's window a few seconds later.

So much for Hope's foresight. She should have gone with the money instead of a hug.

CHAPTER 9

I didn't even think about it. I scooped up the bottles of water and started running. It wasn't long before one car came along, then another. Both understandably ignored my thumb. We weren't that far from the city limits, and they were women driving alone. Only a psycho or a guy who'd been left for dead—possibly for good reason—would be out running in the desert heat. The best I could hope for was that they'd call the cops.

My company cell phone was in the damn limo, confiscated by Tony as a perk that was no longer necessary. He obviously had no problem thinking ahead.

I knew Hope probably wasn't in any danger, but all I could think about was getting to her. Well, that and how many different ways I could kill Tony.

Another car soon approached, and this one sounded like it was slowing down. Lo and behold, it was a beautiful woman in a purple convertible, and, hot damn, she was stopping!

"Going into Flagstaff, I presume?" she asked as I hopped in.

"Yes, ma'am."

"How far did you come on foot?" She looked me over. "It couldn't have been too far, or you'd look like an overcooked hot dog."

We shot forward. She had a lead foot, and I loved her for it.

"Believe me, I'm starting to feel like one." I drank half of one of the waters, trying to determine my options. It had been maybe five minutes, but the limo could be anywhere. "Can I ask you to drop me at the police station?"

"Sure. You okay?"

"No. My ex-boss booted me from a limo and made off with my wife."

The second I said it, I knew I shouldn't have. It was almost as though something had lulled my brain for a moment and out it came. I gathered up my water bottles, figuring I was about to get my ass dumped by the side of the road. Again. At least I was that much closer.

"Was this something your wife wanted to happen?" she asked.

"Not in the slightest."

She nodded and gave me another quick once-over. "I believe you, though you don't seem as upset as you should be. The guy would have to be Adonis to turn her head."

I laughed. "Some would think he is, but she definitely does not. Honestly, I think he's in more danger from her than the other way around," I admitted with pride. "What's your name?"

"Lily."

"Thank you for helping me, Lily. You're very kind, as well as beautiful." I complimented her back.

"Not always." She sighed, and I felt a wave of great sadness come over me. "Hey, is that your limo up ahead?"

I sat up straighter in my seat. We'd reached the beginnings of civilization, including stop lights. The limo holding my wife was indeed sitting at a light that was about to turn green. "Yes, it is. I'll hop out at the next light if you can get closer."

She flipped a button and the top began to pull up over the convertible. "You could lose them on foot, and he'd be onto you. How about if I stay on them until we hit a better opportunity?"

"Words aren't enough, but again, thank you." I looked over at her, moved beyond mere gratitude.

"True love will prevail."

I'd heard it put like that before, but where? There wasn't time to dwell on it as we breezed through the same green light, but were stopped at the next intersection. The limo was at a red light up ahead. I wasn't worried about the lights. Flagstaff was small, and I knew it somewhat from the exploring we'd done when we'd arrived in Arizona. Unfortunately, it could be that they were dumping my stuff somewhere and heading on to Sedona. I highly doubted my new guardian angel was headed there, or would be willing to go that far.

We were on the move again and the limo suddenly picked up speed. Had they somehow made us? I wasn't sure, but game over. The second we were close enough, I was going for it.

They took the last turn with a screech of tires, and my heart jumped into my throat. They'd pulled in to the emergency room of a hospital. I didn't have to tell Lily to step on it. We arrived with our own screeching tires as the driver's door and a back door of the limo swung open.

I was out of the car before it came to a complete stop, running for the limo and calling my wife's name.

Hope emerged from the back, every beautiful inch of her intact. There were groans coming from the limo, masculine, but with an oddly high pitch. I got some answers when the driver helped Tony, doubled over in pain, out of the limo and into the ER.

"How did you get here?" Hope ran into my arms and held me tight.

I held on a little longer before pulling back to point out Lily. "I hitched a ride. Do I need to ask what happened to Tony?"

"My foot slipped."

I thought about how those Doc Martens had felt on my toes, through my boots, and I couldn't help wincing.

She grinned at me. "And then my knee, and my elbow after that."

I started to laugh. How ironic that Tony was now doubled over with the kind of pain I was supposed to be feeling, and I was standing there with Hope in my arms feeling nothing but love.

Zeus must have had his attention diverted, and I could venture a guess where.

"Let's get out of here," I said.

We popped the trunk and grabbed our stuff, but didn't bother moving the limo or taking the keys out of the ignition. We were no longer employees.

The convertible pulled up, top down once more. "Hop in," Lily offered. She didn't have to say it twice.

"Where are you lovebirds headed?"

I had no idea. Worse, I had no means. The corporate credit card had been handed over with the corporate cell phone, and I had no powers to conjure up a single penny.

Hope reached into her pocket and took out a slip of paper. She rattled off an address as I stared and Lily laughed. Hope handed me the paper. "It's from Gary, our limo driver."

I'm sorry. I couldn't tell you his plans, but I knew you'd hold your own. He had me book a suite here for tonight to…well, you know to what. I secretly booked and prepaid another room under Mond and Nona Yerbesnis.

I said the names out loud and started laughing too. The note went on to list the address that Hope had rattled off. I should have known. The majority of humans were good, or at least wanted to be good. For them, hugs because they were doing the right thing was worth more than money.

It took a little more than ten minutes to get to the hotel, which turned out to be more like a resort on the edge of the city. It was doubtful Tony would be hobbling anywhere but back to his motorhome, but if he did show up at the resort, the setup meant it was unlikely we'd run into him.

I was sorry to say goodbye to Lily, and she seemed sad to say goodbye to us. I'd felt oddly comfortable with her, and sensed that big wave of sadness from earlier was more a permanent state. I wished we could help her as she'd helped us, but other than accepting heartfelt hugs as payment, she was quick to leave.

It had been an eventful day, and it wasn't even noon yet. Hope and I ate an early lunch in the hotel restaurant and were lucky enough that our room was ready soon after. I appreciated any extra time I could get, and I intended to make every minute of it count.

The room was very nice, but my gaze was on my wife. I wanted her naked and inviting on the King-sized bed.

As soon as the image hit my brain, I gasped in pain. Prometheus's warning flashed like a neon sign. Don't. Come.

Right. Yeah, sorry bro. I loved the guy and missed him like Hades, but his timing sucked. Coming was definitely on the agenda.

This wasn't about what I wanted, not that I didn't want it with every fiber of my being. No matter what, I couldn't let Hope think I didn't want to make love with her. She would be hurt when I disappeared, but I had a plan. I figured I could create my death in her mind. I knew firsthand how much that would suck, but at least she'd know she was both loved and desired.

I was proud of myself for thinking of it, even if it was technically born from hindsight. Wasn't that learning from my mistakes?

Bottom line, nothing was going to stop me from making love with my wife.

CHAPTER 10

"Who do you see when you look at me like that?"

What? The question brought me back to the present, where Hope was still dressed and standing in front of the bed instead of on it. She was also frowning.

I closed the distance between us and caressed her soft cheek. "You."

"You called for Pandora when you ran toward the limo earlier. I'm not mad," she clarified before kissing my palm. "I know you're kind of obsessed with ancient Greek mythology. I just want to make sure you're here with me. That you know I'm flesh and blood Hope, a human who makes mistakes."

"Don't you get it? Pandora was a human gift from the gods." I closed my eyes against a wave of emotion before being able to look at her to say the words. "I'm not mixing you up with some idea of perfection. I'm calling you, Hope, a gift beyond value. Faults and all."

She was quiet for a moment before she nodded.

"From anyone else, that would border on stalker scary. From you, it makes sense."

I laughed. "Thanks. I think."

"Will you do something for me now, though?" She licked her lips in a nervous gesture that made me want to beg for mercy.

"Yes." It didn't matter what she asked for, it was hers.

"Will you take your clothes off first this time?"

I stepped back and stripped without another word, or even a wince at leaving my pain-free zone. When I was done, I laid her hands on my bare chest.

"Please," I took a deep breath. "Touch me."

"Jack." It was a whisper of desire. It was also the wrong fucking name.

"Please don't get mad." I put my hands over hers, afraid she'd pull away. "But that's not my name. The Powers That Be thought I should go in under a fake name, and I'll bet I can thank Tony for coming up with that one."

"Thank god!" Her topaz eyes danced with humor. "So what is your real name?"

I couldn't give her that, but it didn't really matter beyond not calling me Jack. "Theus." I settled on getting as close to my real name as I dared. "Yeah, I really am Greek."

I kissed her, both to stop any more questions and because I really, really wanted to kiss her. It was all good until her soft palm slid down my body.

The next thing I knew, I was over her on the bed and she was pushing at my chest. "Theus, don't you dare!"

The first time she used the name was in warning, dammit.

"Shit! Sorry!" I forced myself to roll to my back. "That was an out-of-control thing, not a trying-to-control thing, I swear."

"Are you saying I need to tie you up?" she asked, clearly hopeful.

Oh fuck. We'd done that once. I still maintained it had resulted in a major earthquake credited to Poseidon. I groaned and covered my eyes with my arm. "Not helping!"

I felt her leave the bed. While the instant return of pain helped get me back under control, I had to wonder if I'd blown it after all. I couldn't look, even when I heard the unmistakable sound of a suitcase zipper. Thankfully, it wasn't long before I felt the bed dip with her weight.

When the movement stopped, I took a deep breath and let my arm fall to the sheets to clutch them in desperation. The only thing Hope was wearing was a look on her face that said she planned to eat me alive.

The next few minutes were delicious agony. Gentle touches that started at my brow, each caress followed by a soft kiss and a quick flick of her hot tongue. I let her draw it out for as long as I could, knuckles white on the sheets, body trembling out of control by the time she dipped below my rib cage. She was methodical in her torture, following a path that took her down the outside of one leg and up the inside of the other.

I'd dare any man to keep his cool when his lover spreads his legs and nips the tender insides of his thigh, let alone when that was followed by a hot flick of tongue. I was a mere man, and glad for it at that moment. Who knew what could have been unleashed with my normal energy.

She gave my other thigh the same nip and lick, but this time her tongue remained on my skin, flicking closer and closer to her true target.

"Ah, gods!" I couldn't let her do it. One touch and I would come, and quite possibly disappear. If that happened before we made love, she would be emotionally destroyed.

Herculean effort my ass. Herc had nothing on what it took for me to release the bedsheets and grasp her hands. She looked startled, then wary. I knew what she was thinking, and that I had to talk fast.

"Please," I rasped. "Can I be inside you the first time? After that—" I swallowed hard. "After that, it can be your mouth. Every damn day, if you want."

That made her smile. "I'll bet." Her fingers tightened in mine. "But I understand what you're saying about the first time, and I'd like that too. Theus, I…I love you. You said it before, but I didn't. I want you to know that before our first time."

Everything in me instantly calmed and filled with warmth. "I love you too."

She took an audible breath. "You're glowing again."

"Damn straight."

I pulled her up and into my arms and rolled us over. Not many couples got a second chance to recreate their first time together. She wasn't a virgin this time, but I refused to dwell on that other than being grateful she wouldn't feel any pain.

I couldn't wait. Gods, she was so beautiful. I felt like I was drowning in those topaz eyes, letting my own love shine right back while I positioned my cock. She was hot and wet, so ready for me to make that first deep thrust.

"Wait!"

I was so far gone that it took a second to register what she'd said. After all of the times I'd stopped her, she was calling a halt at that moment?

"Wait?" I asked, incredulous.

She nodded. "Safety girl, remember? Condom?"

Shit. I groaned, fighting the need to continue. It wasn't about safety, though she had no way of knowing that. But I could get her pregnant. Gods, to have her belly rounded with our child…

No! I fought my instincts with everything I had and managed to roll away yet again. I couldn't do that to her. To them. Chances were too high she'd be raising our child by herself. Watching over them would not be enough.

"Give me a few minutes and I'll go see if they sell them in the main building," I muttered. "I'm sorry. I didn't plan this. Hades, that's the problem, isn't it? I didn't think ahead. I kind of suck at it—er, the thinking ahead part, not the sex part," I clarified, just in case there was any confusion.

"Good thing that's my greatest strength. The thinking ahead part, and the sex part."

I turned toward her. She was grinning and holding up a strip of condoms. "They were in my suitcase. The last thing you said before we left for Flagstaff was that you wouldn't hurt me, and that you love me. I believed you."

She had opened a packet and tossed the rest of the strip aside as she spoke. I reached for it.

"You don't want me to do the honors?" she asked.

I shook my head. "I'm not giving away one second of any self-control I have left."

I had never used a condom, and I fumbled a little, but it was a mere twenty seconds until I had the damn thing on and every bit of Hope back under me, right where we'd left off. Her slick, smooth heat wasn't as intense on the crown of my cock, but that was okay. It didn't lessen the moment, and under the circumstances, I considered it helpful to have even a miniscule less risk of embarrassing myself.

I framed her face with my hands, holding her gaze as I slowly but firmly pressed deep. We were both breathing hard and trembling by the last inch.

"Okay?" I whispered. Her eyes were wide and she looked a little stunned, making me wonder if she was as ready as I'd thought. "It's all right. I can try to take it slow." I stroked her cheeks with my thumbs. "I love you. No matter what happens, I love you. I always will."

As soon as I said it, I was suffused with heat. I could actually see my hands glowing against her face, and I could feel that heat everywhere.

Everywhere.

"Oh my god!" she cried. Her eyes snapped shut and she shook harder, arching against me.

I caught my breath at the first clench around my cock. A rush of liquid heat bathed me with the next squeeze, pushing that breath out of me on a groan. I don't remember when I started to move. I was making long, deep strokes, my forehead pressed to hers, our breath and cries entwining along with our bodies. The heat kept climbing inside and out, racing up my spine, stroking my cock with each thrust until I thought I would go insane trying to maintain control, waiting for—That!

A groan tore from me, nearly painful in its

intensity as Hope clutched my shoulders and stiffened. I wanted to watch her and pulled back as far as I could in her grasp, only to get the shock of my immortal life.

Hope was glowing too.

The liquid heat became an unbearable pleasure suspended between us as I surged forward one last time, then it burst back down my spine and returned to her with the power of a lightning bolt from Zeus. I could feel myself blacking out as I had when Hypnos had put his hand on my shoulder.

This was it, then. The big goodbye.

Hope! I struggled to consciousness, my heart pounding so hard it felt like blows from Hephaestus' hammer. Then I felt the rise and fall of her chest beneath me and groaned in relief. Whatever had happened, we were both there, in the hotel room, still joined.

I pulled out and took care of the condom, grateful to find it hadn't melted. Then I came back over her, wanting my face to be the first thing she saw when she came to. I could feel the presence of several animals in the distance and way more energy coursing through me than I had in months.

I was no longer merely human.

I swallowed a lump of fear as Hope's eyes slowly opened.

"Epimethius," she breathed my name.

It was sweet to hear my full name on her lips, sweeter still that she remembered our game at that moment. Then I looked, really looked. It wasn't a game.

Pandora gazed back at me, love shining bright. She

touched my face and said my name again.

"Pandora?"

She nodded, tears coming to her eyes. By the gods, my own tears were streaming down my face. "Do you remember everything?" I asked. "Us being Jack and Hope too?"

When she nodded again, I slowly filled her in on what I knew. Other than a cry of dismay when I got to the part about why I had tried not to sleep with her, she didn't say a word until I finished.

"I don't want to lose you again." She reached up and stroked my cheek. "I've lived so many lives without you. They've been…hollow. I always felt like something was missing."

"Me too. I can't lose you again, Pandy."

The last thing either of us expected was to hear a third voice in the mix. "You don't have to. I told you true love would prevail."

Pandora gave a short scream and I jerked so hard I nearly found myself buried in her again.

"Oh, for the love of Me," Lily said. "Get a hold of yourselves."

She was sitting next to us on the bed, back to the headboard, and she'd dropped whatever spell she'd used that kept me from recognizing her. Lily wasn't Lily of the purple convertible rescue team. She was Hera, Queen of Mount Olympus and wife of Zeus.

"Oh." Pandora nodded, understanding everything without needing it spelled out.

I only had about half the alphabet, with some key letters missing. I was also not thrilled about having company in our bed, especially while we were still naked and the clock was ticking.

Hera rolled her eyes. She snapped her fingers and

Pandora and I were fully dressed, sitting together on the small couch. Hera was apparently comfortable where she was, having conjured up a nail file. I'd always hated when she dove into my head, but I knew better than to say anything. That came from centuries of hindsight too. Hera was one powerful woman.

Pandora took one look at me and started laughing. I looked down. I was wearing a white T-shirt with a picture of Hera on a throne and a caption that read Love Conquers All.

"You and Pandora are safe for eternity now," Hera said, her attention still on her nails. "You may each ask one question."

"How?" Pandy asked before I could say anything. She was brilliant. That one little word covered a lot of ground.

Hera's lips turned up in a small smile. "I know my husband's strengths, and his weaknesses. Once given, he will keep his word as ruler. It's getting him to give his word that's difficult. Well, that and keeping his dick in his robes." She shrugged and blew on her index finger.

I tried not to think about the sadness I had sensed in Lily. That alone should have been warning that I was dealing with Hera. It clung to her like a scent.

She looked directly at me with a raised brow. "Do not hide that you care about others, Epimetheus. That is the why of it. The how of it was by issuing a challenge to my husband. You see, Pandora was not part of your initial punishment. I bet your future that true love would prevail, no matter the obstacle in its path."

"So Prometheus was given the opposite information on purpose?" Pandora squeezed my hand, but it was too late. I had asked my question. Crap, but it wasn't like I could ask Hera about Dionysus's fate. She'd wanted him dead since the day he was born.

Hera rolled her eyes again. "Get real. That wasn't Prometheus in Las Vegas any more than I was Lily in Arizona. Zeus was feeding you information."

She sat up and looked at Pandora. "I know the question you were thinking, and yes, you will both live on Mount Olympus." Then she turned that gaze to me. "Here's another freebie. You and Pandora are safe for now. Try not to piss Zeus off again. Oh, and *never* fuck with a goddess scorned."

She disappeared, the nail file falling to the bed with a soft plop.

The next thing I knew, Pandora and I were in bed, naked again, as Hera had found us. Except it was our marriage bed, in our home on Mount Olympus.

I kissed my wife and entered her nice and deep in one stroke. "No more safety girl, and no opening gift jars *or* boxes," I gasped. Damn, she felt good!

"I'm foresight, you're hindsight," she shot back. Her nails dug into my back and she matched my rhythm, fast and hard. "We make all decisions together."

No argument there.

"It's time to come!" she cried. "Now!"

No argument there either.

"Hindsight?" Pandora murmured, gasping for breath right along with me.

Great Zeus, that had been fast and hard. "Too quick. We need to do it again."

"Good thing we have eternity."

EPILOGUE
(1 YEAR LATER)

I had learned very quickly upon my return to Mount Olympus that I could not ask about Dionysus. I thought about him every day, especially as my self-imposed time limit approached to wait for him, so I could punish Tony and Juice.

Then, out of the frickin' blue, there he was literally dancing out of Zeus's throne room! We clasped forearms, but I didn't let go when he did.

"What gives?" he asked.

"I thought I might have to hold onto you, so you don't take off in the middle of a conversation."

He had the decency to look guilty. "Look, I'm sorry. I really thought Zeus would follow me and you'd have the sense to disappear."

I rolled my eyes.

"Whatever he did to you, I imagine it was just as awful as what I went through. Maybe worse. Is there any way I can make it up to you?"

I smirked. "Yeah, actually. There is."

EPILOGUE
(5 YEARS LATER)

"Pandy, you're killing me!"

She licked the head of my cock like a lollipop. "That's impossible. Besides, you're the one who said I could do this every day."

"I didn't think you'd—Ahhhh! For the love of… Have you been talking to the Erotes again?"

"Nope." She took me deep, all the way to the back of her throat, then released me with a pop. "I took notes. They did the talking."

I couldn't comment if I had wanted to. She'd taken me to the hilt again, this time adding something indescribable using her tongue. But then I felt her tongue flicking the underside of my cock while something warm and wet still danced on the sensitive head. I wanted to open my eyes, but I also wanted to stay there forever, deep in her throat, having her continue whatever in Hades she was doing.

I could do neither.

There was no time to warn her. One second I was

flying through the universe, the next I convulsed and proved how happy she'd made me.

It was a while before I could loosen my grip on the sheets so I could wrap my arms around her. Returning the favor would have to wait until my heartbeat stopped soaring with Pegasus.

"By the gods, we're lucky," I gasped when I could finally speak.

She slid up my body, settling on her back into the crook of my arm. "That we are. It really did work out the best for everyone, even Hera. Plus, it's like an extra bonus every time we watch Tony on one of those science shows. Though you got a little green toward the end of that one on praying mantises yesterday."

I shrugged. "Snuff films aren't my thing. You know, both Tony and Juice should be as happy about their outcome as we are about ours."

Pandora gave a snort of laughter. "How do you figure that? Every year, Tony reincarnates as a praying mantis and risks getting his head bit off by a female, and wasn't Juice on yet another one of those medical mystery shows for a recurring hemorrhoid the size of a baseball?"

"Yup. They both got everything they ever wanted. Tony is on a show watched by millions, and he does nothing but chase females and have dangerous, unattached sex. Juice has his growth in the record books. He actually got off easy, considering he was supposed to be a hemorrhoid, not have one."

She was laughing hard now, her breasts shivering with the movement. "Somehow, I don't think they see it that way."

"Well, maybe they should have thought ahead," I

said with a smile as I reached down to flick one of her nipples. "And speaking of payback…"

THE END

Thank you for reading GREAT ZEUS! To learn more about me and see what other books I have available, please visit my website, www.DaltonDiaz.com

I love to hear from readers!

Email addy:
Dalton@daltondiaz.com or
DaltonDiazRomance@yahoo.com
Facebook: https://www.facebook.com/dalton.diaz.3
Twitter: https://twitter.com/DaltonDiaz

ABOUT THE AUTHOR

Hmm. I have no idea why people want to know what makes me... me, but here it goes: My favorite hobby is reading, and I am a complete romance snob.

If a story doesn't have romance, it isn't worth it. If there's hot sex, all the better.

Let's face it, fantasy is usually a lot more fun than reality. Not always, but usually. As a writer, one can be anything, do anything, say anything that comes to mind. There are a thousand and one ways to make things happen, each one more exciting than the last.

Since I have a very active imagination, this is the best job in the world.

Oh My God

by
Ashlyn Chase
.

Oh My God

By Ashlyn Chase

DEDICATION

To my loving family on both sides of the veil. Your unconditional love and support have not gone unnoticed.

ACKNOWLEDGEMENTS

Thanks to Dalton Diaz for adding so much more to my simple story and making it a much better book!
And, as always, thank you to my loving husband Mr. Amazing. He truly deserves his nickname for so many reasons.

PROLOGUE

Two Greek gods, friends and partners in mayhem, taunt the wrong goddess whose volcanic temper blasts a whole new island off of Hawaii.

When Zeus finds out, he'll use their own worst nightmares against them.

Epimetheus stays to face his punishment while Dionysus takes off. He's not as big a jerk as that makes him sound. He's sure the powerful God will know who instigated the whole thing and follow, giving his friend time to get away. Zeus will be even angrier, but he has to catch him first!

CHAPTER 1

"Hello, everyone. I can't remember my name, but I think I'm an alcoholic."

The room fell silent. A few titters began in the back, then the chuckles spread and before I knew it, the whole room was guffawing.

"You came to the right place, Mister!" yelled a listener from the back of the room.

I felt my cheeks heat. They must be turning red. Well, fine. At least they'd match my eyes.

The gorgeous young women who'd taken me to this AA meeting slapped their luscious thighs and laughed out loud with the rest of them. If it wasn't for their sex appeal, I'd have stood up and walked out. How humiliating!

I pictured their creamy skin under their jeans. The brunette with big brown eyes would have a bikini tan. The other, an auburn redhead with long, spiral curls, would probably be a sunscreen wearer, but I loved fair complexions too. In fact, I enjoyed pretty much everything about women. It's odd how I knew that about myself but little else since the amnesia.

I elbowed the pretty brunette on my right. "Hey, I came here to get help and everybody's laughing at me."

The young woman, Brenda she said her name was, patted me on the knee and said with a southern drawl, "It's all right, honey. We understand. We're laughin' with you."

"But I'm not laughing."

"Well you should, darlin'. When you're feelin' better, you'll be tellin' your story to the world, and you'll be laughin' too."

The meeting resumed but with my hangover, I couldn't concentrate on what the speakers said. Yet, despite my pounding headache and roiling stomach, I could concentrate on Brenda and Mandy's thighs.

I sensed a passionate nature in both of the women.

Mandy, the redhead, seemed like the quiet type. Like a swan though, she had all kinds of energy underneath the surface.

Brenda liked to touch. I love touchers. Every chance she got she put a hand on my arm or my leg. Now if I can just get her to zero in on the space between them. My jeans grew tighter as I imagined it.

Mandy wagged her top leg continuously, and I could barely keep my eyes off her shapely ankle, graced by a rhinestone anklet. The afternoon light refracted sparkles from it as if fairy dust were being sprinkled all around our legs and feet. Her t-shirt spoke volumes in glitzy rhinestones too. They spelled out 'Half Naughty Half Nice. Which half do you want?' over her ample breasts. I wanted both halves in my mouth, thank you.

You've gotta love New Orleans. Short skirts,

brilliant colors, and lots of glitz were the preferred attire in the French Quarter, especially at Carnival time. That must have been why I was here. Somehow, I just knew I never missed a good party.

Had I lived here for years? Maybe I was just a tourist. Why oh why hadn't I had some kind of ID on me when I fell off that balcony and onto my head last night during Mardi Gras?

The girls, Brenda and Mandy, said I had been leaning over the balcony trying to throw them some beads when they'd flashed their tits at me. They said I must have been pretty drunk because I'd almost fallen off the balcony when a flat-chested girl flashed, but the two of them showing their voluptuous gifts in unison must have been too much. I'd tumbled over the wrought iron railing and landed, *bam*, right on my head.

Fortunately, for me, they'd felt guilty and driven me to the hospital when I'd come to. They'd stayed until the emergency room had kicked me out, then they'd brought me here.

I couldn't wait until the meeting ended. I wanted to take the two of them to a private place to make out. Who was I kidding? I wanted to screw them silly. Maybe Armstrong Park… Now how did I remember the name of a park in New Orleans, but I couldn't come up with my own name? Oh, man, I needed a drink.

Shit. Today was Ash Wednesday. Nine out of every ten people in the meeting had soot on their foreheads. The girls wanted to give up liquor for Lent. They said they did it every year and thought it would be a good idea if I did too. Maybe they were right.

Maybe I was a Catholic. Everyone else seemed to be. And since I didn't know about the other bad habits I had, I'd have to give up alcohol, although I sensed I may have had lots of bad habits.

Oh, thank Zeus. The meeting was almost over. We just needed to stand in a circle and hold hands. I could do that.

Mandy's hands were warm and dry. Brenda's were hot and sweaty, and she'd been flirting with me. Oh, yeah, she was ready to roll. Suddenly, everyone began to recite the Lord's Prayer.

"Our Father, who art on Mount Olymp..." Hey, they had a different version. Oh, well, I'd just listen to theirs and maybe next time I could fake it...

While walking arm in arm with my willing women, my arm 'accidentally' brushed against their big, bouncy breasts. Little things began to come back to me. Nothing important, mind you, like my friggin' name.

Yet, I had flashes of what looked like it might be my everyday life. Scenes of debauchery and excess. Wine, women and song. Damn, it looked like fun. I must have been living the good life in N'awlins, as Brenda called it. But was my life really as good as it looked? I didn't get much out of the meeting, but it seemed as if alcohol had destroyed the lives of dozens of people.

Yet, the girls had mentioned that the key to sobriety was replacing an old bad habit with a healthy new one. I'm so glad we all agreed that sex is one of the healthiest habits out there. It's natural, it's fun, it's good exercise, and regular sexual release keeps that nasty frustration from building up. Hell, if only everybody was too busy fucking to get all pissed off, there'd be no more wars.

Brenda took us to her apartment. We wedged our bodies into her tiny elevator, and my zipper strained against the building lust in my cock. I really couldn't contain myself much longer. As soon as the doors were closed, I attacked Brenda, pushing her against the wall and kissing her hard. Meanwhile, my left hand found Mandy's breast so I grabbed and kneaded it. Mandy groaned in pleasure as my thumb found the large pebble among the small rhinestones, and I rubbed her nipple. How fortunate that they both went braless.

Brenda's breathing grew fast and shallow. I could tell their hearts were beating faster, too. Oh, yeah, I looked forward to a really good time.

It was all we could do to get into the privacy of Brenda's place before we exploded into orgasmic pleasure right there in the hallway. Her hands were shaking while trying to open the door with her key. Oh, dear Zeus. I couldn't wait any longer.

"Open the damn door!" On my words, the door flew open and all three of us tumbled inside.

"Wow, that was weird," Brenda said. "I hadn't even turned the key yet."

I ripped open my shirt without taking the time to unbutton it. Buttons flew everywhere. "Where's your bedroom?" I panted.

"In there!" Brenda pointed and both girls pulled their t-shirts off over their pretty heads as they bounced into the bedroom behind me. All four puckering nipples begged for my attention.

Oh Lord in heaven, hallowed be thy name, thy

kingdom come and so would I, just as soon as—

Whoa. What if I couldn't hold off long enough to satisfy both of them? I wanted my own release, of course, but I had to see the ecstasy on their faces too.

What was I worried about? I could sense my studliness.

We all wriggled out of our jeans at the same time, and I stole a glance at their gorgeous backsides as they whipped off their thongs. When they turned towards me, they gaped at my enormous erection. I raised my eyebrows at their completely bare pussies. When had girls begun shaving their entire pubic areas? Hey, I wasn't complaining. No more little curly hairs in my mouth? That worked for me.

I couldn't help noticing Mandy—her bright, eager smile and taut, round ass up in the air as she jumped onto the bed. Oh, man. She was all woman. Not at all the shy creature she had seemed. Her rhinestone anklet sparkled in the low light.

"Aren't you going to take off that jewelry, Mandy, dear? I don't want it scraping against my back while we're doing it."

"I never take it off. Is that a problem?"

I shook my head. I'd just have to avoid the damn thing. I wasn't about to give up my romp with the glorious redhead.

Meanwhile, Brenda's aggressive nature hinted at a bit of testosterone and that excited the hell out of me, too. She grabbed my cock, stroked it and said, "I can't wait to fuck this monster. I want to be first."

"I've never seen one so big," Mandy said, breathlessly. "But if Brenda's first, then it may be a little less, um, full by the time you get to me, right?"

"Don't worry my lovelies. I'll have plenty for you

both. Meanwhile, Mandy, you can play with it while I kiss and fondle your anxious friend."

"Oh, God, please hurry," Brenda cried.

I grinned. 'Oh, God.' Something about that particular exclamation pleased me. Her legs were already spread wide. I dove on top of Brenda and raised myself to a kneeling position, so Mandy could scoot underneath, face up, and suck my cock. One quick kiss and I went straight to Brenda's breasts. I devoured the right one while balancing on my right elbow. My free hand travelled to her pussy, and I teased the wet folds of her labia while she writhed and moaned.

Meanwhile, Mandy had found my balls and licked them energetically. Oh, Zeus! I savored the electric shudders coursing through me.

I sensed Mandy's tentativeness about taking my huge cock in her mouth. Fine. She'd love its length and thickness as soon as I sunk it inside of her. Somehow I knew a woman would appreciate a good stretch while I connected with her G-spot. In my flashes of memory, it seemed as if I had done a lot of fucking.

Brenda moaned, and as soon as I shifted my attention to her other breast, she clutched my hair. Thank Zeus it's shorter than it appeared in some of my flashbacks. I must have cut it for just this reason. Her moans and arches increased as I suckled harder.

By then she had begun pulling my hair, and I was through playing. Her nether regions were completely soaked. Now, I'd give her what she'd come for. Or what she would come for any second. She began bucking and screaming the minute I rubbed my wet fingers over her clitoris. I pictured fistfuls of my hair being yanked out so I told her to remove her fingers, and I shimmied down to suck and lick her clit.

"Yes, yes!" she cried as her body vibrated. In no time at all she bucked, screamed and convulsed. Meanwhile, Mandy had adjusted and poked her finger in my ass while she licked my dick.

Oh, these girls were great. I'd have to reward each of them with the best orgasms they'd ever have in their lives. And I'd have plenty, myself, by the time the night was through.

Brenda pushed at me, and in a weak voice she begged, "No more. Oh, God, please, I can't take any more."

That's all she needed to say. I rose up and balanced on my knees as I gave her a big sloppy smile, my mouth covered with her juices. "I think you might like to rest a bit while I give Mandy equal treatment."

She nodded, a grateful look in her eyes.

"Mandy, honey, you did a remarkable job on my balls. Once Brenda recovers, maybe she'll suck my cock for me. I want to be hard as a spike when I screw both of you.

Brenda smiled and nodded enthusiastically. Apparently, she couldn't talk yet. She breathed as if practicing Lamaze.

I told Mandy to show me her beautiful ass, and she kneeled in front of me. Oh, dear Zeus, I loved her in that position. I fondled her soft bottom first, then cupped and squeezed her beautiful, natural tits while I rubbed my cock up and down her ass crack. Brenda said she was ready to go down on me, so I flipped over and told Mandy to sit on my face while I licked her to heaven. She complied happily.

Brenda hardened my erection to cast iron with her slow, steady rhythm. "Oh… I love that, Brenda. Keep it up."

"Pun intended?" Mandy asked.

Ha! Cute and bright. Oh, yes. I'd get her off as if she had been launched by NASA.

I parted her pussy lips with my tongue and buried it inside her core, listening to her groan as I fucked her with my long tongue.

Meanwhile, Brenda had increased the speed and suction, so I had to take some deep breaths through my nose and hope I wouldn't hyperventilate. I moved my mouth to cover Mandy's clit. As I licked and sucked her, she came, and came, and came in earth shattering cries. My word, but the quiet one could scream! My mouth dripped with her liquids down both sides of my face. At last, when she quieted, she pulled herself away and collapsed, facing the foot of the bed.

"Oh, finally!" Brenda seemed mighty excited. "Where do you want me?"

"I want you on top, Brenda baby."

She straddled me and hovered over my cock. Her anxious eyes and deep breath betrayed her trepidation about the fit. At last, she sunk down on it, and we both moaned in bliss. Mandy struggled up onto one elbow and watched me fuck her friend with fascinated interest.

Brenda gurgled and moaned and threw her head back. We mated in a savage rhythm, the brave girl bouncing up and down on top of my engorged erection. For some reason, I felt able to control my rod's movements even though I was ready to shatter. I made sure my cock touched the sweet spot inside her cavern, and we both went crazy.

She bucked, as if riding a wild stallion, which in a way, she was.

"Oh God! Oh God!" she cried. I allowed myself to orgasm after Brenda had crashed over the edge. I pulled out and shot into space, releasing my copious cum.

Brenda tumbled off and lay on the other side of me in a limp heap and I wondered if she had passed out. Maybe she had. Well, at least she was still breathing. She wheezed like an asthmatic.

"Mandy, my sweet, lick your friend's honey off my cock, and as soon as we're all revved up, I'll take you doggy style."

"Ugh. Lick off Brenda's cum? That's kind of disgusting. I'd rather not."

"Oh. I guess it never occurred to me that it might be distasteful since I have both of your fluids all over my face…"

"How about if I wipe you off with my hand?" She winked.

"Sure, baby. That'll work too."

She worked me up into a dither with a fantastic hand job. Soon, I was ready to go again and anxious to bury my big cock in her little hole. I grabbed her chin and shapely warm body and pulled her towards my mouth. Electricity simmered between us as we shared a deep, passionate, French kiss. Our tongues were like toys, and we played with each other…One hiding and the other seeking. We played with our bodies too. I kneaded and squeezed her tits, and she pulled and squeezed my penis. A delightful suction had built up in the fusion of our mouths.

Surprisingly, kissing Mandy beat the hell out of

kissing Brenda. My tongue just couldn't stop teasing the inside of her mouth. She seemed to take pleasure in kissing me back, darting her tongue over and past my lips, mating, swirling, sucking…

Who knew that a simple kiss could make me so hot?

Maybe she just knew how to lay one on me. I could get used to this. At last, we managed to pry ourselves apart, already panting. Both of us on fire, we needed completion more than oxygen and were going to fuck savagely. She positioned herself on her hands and knees in front of me.

Dear Zeus, I wanted to fuck this little filly more than I'd ever wanted anything in my life…I think. I had no idea what I might have wanted in the past, but I sure as hell wanted this now. I was in danger of ramming my rod right into her.

I couldn't help noticing she trembled, though.

"Mandy, sweet angel. I know you're a little afraid of my enormity, but don't worry. We'll fit just fine. I'll be gentle. You'll see."

She visibly relaxed and turned her head to smile at me. "Okay. I'll tell you if it hurts." Concern suddenly sobered her expression. "You'll stop, won't you? If it hurts, I mean?"

I stroked her soft butt cheeks and said, "Of course, I will, darling." Damn, I wanted to fuck her so badly, I'd have said anything. So fine, innocent and willing. I had to have this one even if I had to fold my member in half.

I tested her wetness. She was well lubed and ready.

I entered her slowly. She groaned but in a welcoming way. Her passage hugged my cock. So tight and so desirable. I let out a long moan and managed to pull back as gently as I entered.

Brenda stirred and opened her eyes just as I found my rhythm with Mandy. Oh good. Now she could watch. I reached around and played with Mandy's clit, and she growled in a thoroughly sexy way through her teeth. Soon she was arching her back and moaning louder and louder.

My own sexual pleasure built to a lofty peak. Mandy gasped, panted and yelped into her bliss. She quivered all over and began to spasm just as I reached my climax. I ejaculated inside of her. My finger kept up the frantic stimulation on her clit.

She was convulsing and screaming. Shuddering and screaming. Clenching and screaming. She climaxed so ferociously I felt like cheering, 'Go, Mandy, go'!

Or should that be 'Come, Mandy, come'?

Either way, she gasped and screamed in a more prolonged orgasm than I thought possible. Dear Zeus. I hoped it wouldn't kill her.

"Oh, God! Oh, God! Oh, God!" she cried.

Poor thing would probably have laryngitis after this. At last, she fell onto the pillow she had been clutching with a whimper. Brenda's eyes were as big as camera lenses, and she blinked, as if taking pictures.

Mandy relaxed there, limp and damp. I ran my hand over my favorite ass in the world, or at least in the room, and asked if she was all right. She giggled.

In a weak rasp, she replied, "Thank you— whatever your name is."

I chuckled. "Why don't you call me 'God'? It seems you both like to use that name with me anyway."

Brenda's shock passed once her friend appeared to have survived the experience. "Ha, we might call you that in bed but not in public."

"Who says we're going out together in public?" I quipped.

Brenda looked hurt. "Me. Us. Aren't we going to hang out together? What about AA?"

"I don't need it. I'll be fine on my own. Besides, I'd like to walk around the city and see if anyone recognizes me."

This tart wasn't quite getting the picture. I had planned to love 'em and leave 'em. I mean, I sensed that's what I usually did.

In my flashbacks, I saw myself fucking hundreds of women at orgies, in alleys, under tables. If women weren't available, men would do, but I'd seen no repeats in my flashbacks yet.

Still I wouldn't mind making love to that minx, Mandy, again. There's nothing like being appreciated for your talents. She had given me a loud and enthusiastic standing 'O'.

Brenda slowly rose off the bed. Her eyes flashed fire and her nostrils flared. "How dare you?" she yelled. "You used us. Now you're just going to get dressed and go?"

CHAPTER 2

"Well, no. I'd planned on staying the night. I could pleasure you both for a few more hours before I have to leave."

"Oh yeah?" Brenda leaned forward and jammed her hands on her hips. "I don't think so, Mister. It's bad enough you don't want to associate with us after screwing us in front of each other, which we let you do out of the goodness of our hearts and future memories, but to come right out and admit it was a one night stand?" Her voice screeched into a high pitched crescendo.

I propped myself on my elbow and puzzled over her curious reaction.

"So, you're telling me that I shouldn't be honest about further involvement? I should make you believe I'll be back to pleasure you whenever you like. Be your booty call? Maybe even lie and say, 'I'll call you' when, clearly, I don't know if I will or not?"

Brenda's face reddened, and she looked like she might explode when Mandy intervened.

"Brenda, relax. He doesn't owe us anything. It's not like we had an understanding or a commitment or anything."

"So you're fine with this?" she screamed. "You don't mind letting a pig fuck your brains out knowing the whole time it's just to get his rocks off then disappear?"

"Well, we knew what would take place. We went into it voluntarily. And we didn't ask for more than sex, did we?"

"Who asks for a commitment before they screw?"

Brenda made absolutely no sense to me whatsoever. Fortunately, Mandy seemed to have her head on straight.

"Well, to be honest, Bren, lots of people do."

"But that never works. Men don't stay interested unless you give 'em a little somethin' somethin'. Now he's gone and made us into sluts!"

Mandy shook her head. It seemed useless to argue, so I reluctantly hauled my contented body from the bed and picked up my clothes. Mandy did the same. Brenda stormed off, letting Mandy and I get dressed.

We stole a glance at each other while wiping up with some Kleenex from the nightstand and Mandy said, "I'm sorry about that. She and I have never done this before. I guess we should have talked about it first."

"It's not your fault. You were great. You shouldn't apologize."

We struggled into our clothes with semi-sticky legs. After she pulled up her zipper, she asked, "So, do you know who you are, yet? Where you live and stuff?"

"No. I keep having these flashbacks but nothing

helpful. I mean, they're very erotic images and that's cool, but I still don't have any idea what my name is or where I might be staying around here."

"He's lying," Brenda yelled from another room. "He knows exactly who he is. He's a pig who pretends to have amnesia so he can get girls to feel sorry for him and take him home. Then he fucks them two at a time! I can't believe I put on a sex show for my best friend! At least, you *were* my friend, Mandy."

"Brenda, don't do this. He screwed us like that because we wanted him to."

Fortunately, I heard the shower start running, and we could talk without being overheard.

"I should probably get out of here. You can do what you want, but I'd advise you to leave, too. I'll bet that girl could scratch your eyes out just for telling the truth and making sense."

"You're right." To my sorrow, Mandy pulled on her glittery t-shirt covering her beautiful bust.

As we left the apartment, I let her step in front of me and followed her down the narrow hallway to the elevator. Hubba, hubba. Her round, little tush swayed back and forth while my mouth watered, again. Was Brenda right? Am I a pig? I hope not because if I am, I think I enjoy being that way. Still, Mandy didn't seem to have a problem with it.

"So, do you have plans?" I found myself asking her. "Anywhere you have to be tonight?"

"Not really. I just thought I'd go home and get some sleep. I have to work tomorrow."

"Not until tomorrow? Well, that's good. There's plenty of time if you want to…um, hang out some more?"

She smiled at me—not the usual polite smile. It denoted a deep understanding of exactly what I meant and delight in my asking. We exited to the street, and her blue eyes sparkled and glowed in the light of the gas lamps lining the sidewalk.

"I could…"

"Great!" I shoved her up against the brick building, thrust my anxious hands over her tits and kissed her hard. She returned the kiss, but only for a moment before she pushed me away.

"I—I think we need a couple of ground rules, first," she said, looking nervous.

"Like what?" I held my breath and prayed she didn't want to turn into a nice girl all of a sudden.

"I have kind of an issue with you. First, I want you to know I just had the best sex of my life."

I nodded. "Okay, that doesn't sound so bad." What the hell? Were all women impossible to please?

"It's just that…" She slipped her arms around my neck and pulled herself close. Her nipples brushed against my chest, and I caught my breath. "It's just that this threesome with my best friend was an experiment. I liked it and could handle it—once. I figured we would have one wild night for our memories in our old age. But I can't get into the idea of sex in front of other people on a regular basis."

"Oh, sure, I understand. But don't you find that a little exhilarating? The idea of someone watching you fuck, er, make love?"

She smiled and looked at the sidewalk. "Sort of, but I was a little embarrassed, too."

"You didn't seem to mind watching as I gave your friend her satisfaction."

She rubbed my biceps as she talked. Her

expression appeared serious but neutral. Maybe she's a research scientist or something?

"No, I didn't. I was curious. I'm glad she went first, though. I was a little nervous about your size. I enjoyed watching, and she was completely okay with having me watch. At least, I thought so at the time."

Oh shit. I was hard as a rock again.

"I like to know what to expect," she continued. "I think all women do. Maybe that's why Brenda got so mad because she expected the wrong thing."

"I love how honest you are. And I'm going to be completely honest with you, angel." I cozied up to her ear and whispered, "That was the best sex of my life, too."

She grinned, and as she kissed me, I congratulated myself for allaying her fears so successfully. How did I know if that was the best sex I had ever had? Don't get me wrong, it was absolutely fantastic. I loved it. But, if I went by what I knew for sure about my life, I'd have to say it was the only sex I'd ever had. Who could tell what I was remembering? Maybe I was just watching reruns of 3-D sex shows in my brain. But it felt so real. Maybe I was a porn star?

When I thought about it, I had to admit that some of those flashbacks were pretty strange. People in togas wearing olive branches around their heads? It must have been a costume party. Some party, though. I'd had two or three lovely ladies all over me at once, biting, licking and fucking me senseless.

Mandy's pink complexion grew pinker, and she gazed up into my eyes. "Would you like to come home with me? We could have a nice time, just the two of us. Don't you think?"

Think? With all the blood rushing out of my brain?

"Of course we could. You do mean 'have sex', don't you?"

"Absolutely."

"Thanks, I'd love to."

Mandy's place was nice. She lived in the Garden District in one of those grand homes with white columns. Of course, she lived in an apartment on the third floor over a nosy landlady and there was no elevator, but what the hell? We had spent most of the trolley ride making out in the back so we practically floated up the stairs. That girl could kiss. Maybe she couldn't put my cock in her mouth yet, but I'd be patient and teach her how. Soon, she'd be sliding her full lips up and down my shaft like a sex machine.

Mandy and I undressed each other in her kitchen. We had stopped to get a drink. We only had fruit juice, I swear. No alcohol. I meant what I had said about giving up booze for the forty days of Lent.

I unzipped and yanked down her jeans while she was reaching into the cabinet for glasses. I had to work the jeans over her rhinestone anklet so it didn't get caught and break. She seemed to think it was special, and I wondered who had given it to her.

She giggled, slapped the glasses on the counter and whirled around. First, she liberated me of my button-less shirt, then while she sucked my nipples, she unzipped my jeans and worked them down to my knees. I bent over to finish taking them off. As I stood up, I grabbed her sparkly t-shirt and whipped it over her head.

Then I shoved her up against the fridge and cupped her ass as I kissed her senseless. Those little magnet things were falling off the fridge all over the floor. My fingers wandered into her thong and pulled the fabric aside while I fingered her already wet pussy. We weren't even horizontal and we were already rounding third base.

She grabbed my cock and used her magic hand to make the valiant soldier stand ramrod straight. Oh, dear Zeus, I couldn't wait to ram my rod right into her anxious, hot sheath.

I broke the kiss to suck her lush, succulent breasts while I worked the thong down until she pulled one high-heeled sandal out of it. Oh, man. She was quivering and moaning already. I had to bury my cock in her, soon.

I grabbed her soft, round bottom, lifted her and pressed her ass against the refrigerator door and without protest, she wrapped her legs around me. Her sweetness was wet, open and inviting me in. This time I wasn't quite as gentle. My cock found her hole like it was a North Pole magnet and there was a South Pole version behind her on the refrigerator door saying, 'Take me. Take me now!' We were pulled together with what could only be called compelling force.

She gasped as I plunged in, then let her breath out on a sigh.

"Are you all right, my sweet?"

"Oh, yes. Do me, please," she said.

"I want to hear you say it right."

She opened her eyes and looked at me in obvious bewilderment. "What?"

"As long as I understand exactly what you want, Mandy. Do you want me to fuck you?"

I pulled out slowly and sunk back in even more slowly. "I want to hear you say, 'Fuck me. Fuck me, darling, fuck me.'"

She moaned as I slid in to the hilt. Then she leaned back and closed her eyes, squinting hard. "Dear, God. Fuck me. Do it!"

"All right, yes. I certainly will."

I took her with long slow strokes until she was continuously moaning and groaning with sexual pleasure. Then I upped the speed and power of my thrusts, hitting her clit harder each time. When I sensed she was close, I really went for broke. Soon she was vibrating in my arms and screaming out my great, new nickname.

"Oh, God! Dear God! Oh, oh, oh…" Her body shook hard, and it was all I could do to keep her from knocking me off balance. Then I came with great jerks and spurts. At least, I finished before we both fell on the hard, linoleum floor.

When I stopped laughing, I asked, "Thirsty now?"

She looked through heavily lidded eyes where fire still smoldered. "More than ever. You got anything left for me to drink?"

I woke up the next day underneath Mandy's red, satin sheet and had a hard time finding my way out. I smiled as I remembered why I was upside down and under the covers. That girl was full of surprises. As it turned out, I didn't need to teach her a thing.

I heard the shower running and remembered she had to work. Bummer. Then I wondered if I had a job somewhere and was AWOL. Had anyone missed me yet? What did I do for a living? Salesman? I seemed able to sell Mandy on just about anything I wanted to do.

Work was something I had to look into, but I wasn't all that anxious to find any. I was enjoying myself. If I found out I had responsibilities, especially if they were pure drudgery—well, I just wouldn't think about that yet. But if my memory didn't return, I would have to get a job. I didn't want to mooch off anyone for too long.

Ah, the shower stopped. Should I walk in and surprise her? As I was getting to my feet, I realized that I could easily wear out my welcome if not my hostess. Besides, it was really time to hit the road. We'd had a good time, but I needed to show my face around town and see if anyone recognized it. I'd find that balcony I fell off of in the French Quarter later, after the parties started.

Mandy popped her towel-wrapped head into the bedroom. In a long, pink robe with rhinestones around the collar and cuffs and a freshly washed face with no makeup, she looked even more innocent. But I knew better.

"Oh, you're up. I'll throw together some breakfast. You must be starving."

I grinned and said, "Yeah. I worked up quite an appetite last night. Have you got a side of beef or a roast pig on hand?"

She giggled in that cute way she had, then said, "I'll find something," and disappeared. I assumed to the kitchen. I went to the bathroom to wash up and dress. Hmmm. My clothes were beginning to smell a bit ripe. I needed to wash, but without a laundry, I improvised. I climbed into the claw-footed bathtub with my jeans and jockey shorts and washed everything in strawberry scented soap. My shirt buttons were gone, so I tossed the shirt in the trash and bathed my armpits. Then I drained the tub, pulled the shower curtain around me and rinsed off in the warm spray. Getting into wet clothes wasn't the easiest thing I've ever done.

I had wrung my clothes out, but still left little puddles trailing behind me on the wood floor as I made my way to the kitchen. I'd just have to dry out in the sun.

"Good morning, beautiful," I said. Mandy was taking corn bread out of the oven. It smelled delicious, and my mouth watered like I hadn't eaten for days. In actuality, I hadn't eaten anything since a donut at the AA meeting. Hmmm. Free food. Maybe I could go to another meeting or two.

"I don't usually eat at home, but I had this in the fridge. I hope it's enough." There was butter, cream cheese, jelly and peanut butter on the table. I piled a bit of everything on a couple of generous slices of hot cornbread and crammed big bites into my mouth before they crumbled.

Her azure eyes grew wide in amusement, but she didn't try to teach me manners, thank goodness. I appreciated her easy-going style. Mandy embodied the meaning of Big Easy.

"So, what are you going to do today?" she asked.

"Dunno." That was all I could mumble around the mouthful.

"I have a few dollars you can have."

I held up my hand and shook my head. She ignored my silent protest and stuffed some one-dollar bills into my jeans pocket. The contact of her fingers through the wet fabric on my thigh sent an electrical signal to my cock. It poked up its head hopefully. Then she found a few quarters and placed them on the table.

"You'll need money for the trolley." She had an uncertain expression on her face and gentled her voice. "Both ways, if you want to come back."

Come back? I hadn't even thought about coming back. Wasn't it time to say 'goodbye' and move on? I took some extra time to think about that while I chewed.

She shrugged. "I mean, you don't have to or anything. I just thought, you know, if you don't have any luck finding out who you are and still don't have a place to stay…"

I finally swallowed and nodded. "Thanks. That's nice of you. I'll, uh, have to see what happens."

She smiled, nodded and looked at her plate. She had buttered her cornbread but added some jelly to it as she spoke. "It was great. Last night, I mean."

"Yeah. It was for me, too." I had the feeling I was supposed to follow up with something like a promise to call or a plan to get together again. I used a diversion.

"So, where do you work, Mandy?"

"At the culinary school in the Warehouse District. It's a nice place. People treat me well, and I eat for free. I get out by four-thirty, usually."

"Sounds good."

"It's boring. I work in the office."

"Oh. Well, I can't thank you enough for your hospitality. And the trolley fare."

She stood. "Do you want a t-shirt? I have a couple of large ones."

"Sure. Do you have the pink one I saw that says, 'I want to be Barbie. The bitch has everything?'"

She giggled, then her expression turned sad. "I'm

going to miss your sense of humor. You're a lot of fun."

With that, she hurried to her bedroom. I felt odd. I wasn't sure what was coming over me. I hadn't experienced this feeling before. At least, I didn't think I had. Damn, it was inconvenient not to know much about myself. I hoped more than ever I'd run into someone who knew me.

Mandy returned with a plain black t-shirt. Size large. It was a snug fit and really stretched out over my chest, but she assured me it made me look hot so I accepted it gratefully. Now the walk to the door and the kiss goodbye. There was that feeling again. Ugh. I didn't like it. Whatever it was, it was unpleasant.

I hoped the discomfort would leave when I did, so I planned to give her a quick peck on the cheek and be on my way. I held her chin between my index finger and thumb for a moment and looked into her eyes. That did it. Her eyes were shimmering, turquoise blue, like the gulf beyond the muddy Mississippi. This woman was different. A breath of fresh air.

She did her best to put on a weak smile. Crap. She was feeling the same thing. I had to get out of there.

"See ya. Thanks for everything" I said. I stuck out my hand, and she put hers in mine accepting an awkward handshake instead of a kiss. Again, she gave me a sad smile but didn't protest.

Dear Zeus, that was it. The feeling was sadness. I hated that feeling! Somehow, I knew that it had to be avoided it at all costs. Now, I understood why. It hurt. Almost physically—right in my chest. I opened the door and charged down the stairs two at a time.

CHAPTER 3

The trolley let me off on Canal Street. I hoped to run into someone I knew in the French Quarter and put this identity issue to rest. At this hour of the morning, Bourbon Street would be fairly quiet. I'd wait until later to visit the balcony I'd plummeted from. Tourists still milled about, and the cafes were full. Maybe I'd find some of the same people I'd partied with Tuesday night. They couldn't all still be sleeping it off, right?

How much money did I have? Not a lot. Three dollars. The trolley had cost a dollar and twenty-five cents. That left me with less than two bucks for lunch if I wanted to save enough to get back to Mandy's place for the night.

Damn. What a decision. Eat? Sleep in comfort later? Become a purse-snatcher? I thought the last one through. Although they'd give me food and a place to sleep if I got caught, prison sex wasn't what I wanted. I didn't want to settle for ugly men in showers when there were so many pretty women in bars.

I bought a pretzel. It's amazing how long a person can make a pretzel last if they're not sure when their next meal might be. I found myself thinking about starving children in other parts of the world. As soon as I had the ability to do so, I'd write a check to alleviate world hunger. Unfortunately, at the moment, I didn't know what name to sign at the bottom.

Uh, oh. Sadness alert! Had to distract myself somehow. I wandered aimlessly and tried to ignore swirls of seagulls eyeing my pretzel. With my head hung low, I bumped into a man who was looking up at the birds. He stopped, studied my face, and his expression turned from annoyance to surprise. "Hey, don't I know you?" he said.

"Yeah, yeah…" I was faking it, hoping he'd come up with the connection if I let him. "You look familiar to me, too. How long has it been?"

"Must be thirty years," he said. "You haven't changed at all."

Thirty years? Who was he kidding? I'd seen myself in a mirror. I looked no more than thirty years old now. Did he remember me from my baby carriage?

He frowned. "No. It couldn't be. You look just like someone I knew in college though. My mistake." Then he smiled and looked like he was drifting off into another, happier time.

"He was quite the party animal. I wonder what ever happened to good old Dennis?" He shook his head as if clearing the picture from his etch a sketch brain. "Sorry."

"That's okay, man," I said, although I was hugely disappointed.

College. That was a thought. Maybe I went to school here? I stopped by a store that was selling local maps and studied one carefully hoping the name of some school would ring a bell. Nothing. Nada. Zip.

I wasted the afternoon walking around a college campus, a music school, and two bookstores. Apparently, I wasn't much for higher learning. The kids on campus looked like—well, kids. I was easily older than most by several years.

Even Mandy was older than college undergrads. I wondered how old she was? I had never asked. I wondered if she had gone to college? And I wondered if I should spend my last buck seventy-five on food or trolley fare.

So far, no one had acted like they recognized me, except for the one gentleman who told me I looked like some kid from thirty years ago named Dennis.

My legs were in good shape, but I had walked all over the friggin' city trying to hang onto that trolley fare. I had to wonder why.

My frustrated efforts were beginning to wear on me. I seemed like such a social guy. Where were all my friends? So far, I had made one friend and one enemy and I had screwed them both. I had to go back to the old city at night despite a bit of apprehension. I was sure that's where I'd find the friends I must have.

What if I didn't have any friends? None at all? Was that why I was holding onto the little money I had and listening to my stomach growl in hunger? I had a sinking feeling there was more to it.

Something about the way my mind kept returning to Mandy bothered me. I was having another feeling I couldn't identify. I kept thinking of her eyes. Her brave refusal to give in to fruitless complaining. Her gifts of kindness, money, even her body. To me—Mr. whoever-you-are. Talk about unconditional!

Okay, it was decision time. Another pretzel or back to Mandy's for a light snack and lots of fucking for dessert? I decided to eat, then that rotten sadness came over me again. As I brooded, I passed a small side street that smelled so good, I had to investigate.

What luck! I burped and rubbed my contented abdomen after having discovered a dumpster behind a restaurant and cooking school. The students must be getting good grades. I'd had some delicious red beans and rice. There were even leftovers that someone must have forgotten to take with them. They were nicely packaged in a Styrofoam container.

Yes, this was the feeling I liked most of all. Belly content. Money in pocket. Woman waiting for fun in bed. Ah, life was good again.

Then I rounded the corner and ran right into Brenda.

She was walking with a guy who looked a bit like her, including some big, man boobs. He towered over me and easily outweighed me by fifty pounds.

Her large eyes rounded, and she pointed at me. "That's him!"

I tried to take a nonchalant approach. "Hey, Brenda. Nice to see you again. I'd love to stay and talk, but…"

Big bruiser interrupted me. "My little sister tells me you took advantage of her and her friend. You're gonna pay for that, Mister."

"Pay? Wouldn't that make her a…"

BAM!

When I came to, Brenda and her 'goon' were gone. So was my money. Crap. Sadness crept in and wedged itself between the throbs of physical pain in my body and left eye. I was pretty sure that would leave a mark.

Knowledge of my identity had not returned. I was hoping that whatever had been shaken loose might have been knocked back into place. But that hadn't happened.

Once I regained my orientation, I noticed dusk was fast approaching. Realizing that the disfigurement I had received from Brenda's brother might interfere with my swift identification angered me, but I had to try anyway.

I rose slowly to my feet and staggered, at first. Someone was coming the other way. I braced myself against the brick building and waited for him to pass. Instead, he slowed down as he came closer. A smile formed on his pudgy face, and he put out his hand.

"Hey there, I know you."

My eyebrows shot up. "You know me?"

"Well, I've seen you. You were at the AA meeting. There's another one tonight. Let me take you there."

"No. Thanks, man. Really. It's just that I have other plans."

"What could be more important than your sobriety?"

"Oh, I don't know. Maybe finding out who I am? Where I live? If I have a job and a family?"

"Still can't remember?"

"No, I can't. But I'm doing fine. Thanks for the offer."

I started to walk away in long, quick strides, but he caught up and walked beside me.

"I hate to say it, but you don't look fine. In fact,

you don't look good at all. Let me help."

I kept going. "I know I look like a mess, but I haven't had a drop of liquor since that meeting, honest."

"Look. You've been beaten up, you have garbage stains all over your clothes, you're homeless, and if you haven't started drinking again yet, that's great, but you probably will."

"You forgot the part about I have no money. Would you have a couple of bucks you could spare?"

The stranger put a hand on my arm, thus stopping my march. He looked at me with sad eyes and said, "I can't do that. You'll spend it on booze. You can come home with me, though. I'm sure my wife would love to give you a hot, home-cooked meal, and I might find you some clean clothes. Then you can sleep on my couch for the night. We can go to AA tomorrow morning. How does that sound?"

I woke up the next morning to the smell of bacon and eggs. Oh, but I was a slave to my stomach. Mrs. L, I believe her name was Marie, got up and prepared a big breakfast for Mr. L and me. His name was Roland L. An odd last name, I thought.

Meanwhile he thought it would be a good idea for me to take a name. Any name. I picked the only name that came to mind.

"Eat up, Dennis. The meeting serves donuts, but you'll need some of Marie's good nutrition if you're going to resist the urge to drink."

"Thanks, I'm starving. Resisting alcohol won't be hard, though. I have a strong constitution."

"We all do, son. Still, you can afford a few

pounds." He patted his rounded belly and laughed. "You've got a long way to go before you look like me."

Thank Zeus for that.

He gifted me with a black leather jacket that he had been keeping for posterity. He said he'd never be able to zip it again and thought I might as well get some use out of it.

As soon as I had eaten and attended another meeting to make this nice guy feel good, I'd be on my way. I wondered why I decided it was important to do this for him, but I didn't have an answer. It just felt like the right thing to do.

Roland lived within walking distance of the meeting, and he thought it would be good for our health to get a little exercise. I just hoped I didn't take up jogging and eating trail mix. I did feel a whole lot better though. A shower, clean clothes, a warm jacket and a good breakfast had done wonders for my mood—until the thought of Mandy crept in.

She had probably hoped to see me on her doorstep when she got home last evening. I could picture the disappointment on her pretty face. Tears may have even rolled down those lightly freckled cheeks of hers. I fantasized about wiping a tear from her peach-soft skin and kissing her cheek. Then letting my tongue slide down her neck and—

Someone came up behind me and spoke in a loud male voice thereby interrupting my magnificent daydream.

"Hey Mister. Be careful of the guy you're with, especially if you have any daughters!"

Damn. It was Brenda's brother again.

"Leave me alone!" I yelled. Suddenly as if on my

command, he turned and fled. That seemed like odd behavior for him.

Roland looked at me with raised eyebrows. "Want to talk about it?"

"No!"

"Suit yourself." Roland stuck his hands in his pockets and kept strolling.

For some reason, I felt rotten yelling at him like that. I could yell at Brenda and her goon of a brother, but Roland was another matter.

"I'm sorry, Roland. I shouldn't have taken my frustration out on you. He deserved it, but you're my—my…"

"Sponsor," he interjected.

"Oh." He looked over and gave me a knowing smile.

Yeah, I guess he had sponsored me last night. His wife stuffed me full of crawfish *etoufette*. Roland washed my jeans and t-shirt and found a coat that used to be his, but now it's mine. How cool was that?

We arrived at the meeting, and Roland began introducing me to people. Since we were early, I chowed down on donuts and coffee and kind of enjoyed my new, er, friends. I had all but forgotten that I might meet an old acquaintance when I felt a hard slap on my back.

"Big D! I don't believe it! What the heck are you doin' here?"

I whirled around and saw a big, bald guy. My age, probably. He was built like a bouncer.

"You know me? Who am I?"

The big guy laughed. Then he scrutinized my face and must have realized I was serious. "You're kiddin' right?"

"No, I'm not. I've been having some, uh, problems with my memory lately. If you know me, please tell me what you know."

He narrowed his eyes and hissed through his teeth. "You're the reason I'm here, asshole."

Roland put a hand on the guy's shoulder. "George, let's keep it constructive. You're both here for the same thing. Recovery."

Bouncer boy took a deep breath and hung his head for a moment. Then he looked me in the eye and said, "Look, I'm sorry if I offended you, but do you really want to know the truth about yourself? I'd better warn you, you might not like what you hear."

This caught me off guard. I finally found someone who knew me, and instead of telling me what a great guy I was, he called me an asshole.

I looked to Roland, and he put his other hand on my shoulder creating a bridge between us. "We've all done things in the past that we're not proud of. I know how ashamed I was when I finally remembered everything I'd done. Marie had already thrown me out of the big bed, and I was about to lose my place on the couch too. I put that poor girl through hell."

Mandy popped into my mind.

"It's possible that our friend is blocking things he's not ready to handle yet, George. Why don't you tell him basics, like his name and where he lives if you know? Things like that."

George shrugged. "We called him 'Big D.' I don't know where he came from or where he went at the end of the day—or the beginning of the next day, more accurately."

"So, you don't know me well. Maybe I'm a nice guy, and you caught me on a bad day."

"Bad day? Honest to God, I've never seen anyone able to drink so much, eat so much, or screw so many women during the same night in my life."

"Big D, huh? Is that all you can tell me about my name?"

"That's it. The women nicknamed you. I'm pretty sure it was because…"

I coughed. "That's okay. I think I can guess." Ambivalence was coursing through me and forcing me into a swirl of emotions.

"Is there anyone who knows me and likes me? Maybe even cares about me?"

He shrugged and shook his head. "I don't know. I don't think so."

Another flashback popped into my brain, and I saw more depraved activity. A naked man and woman and anyone wanting a turn at them taking one. They looked pretty drunk but didn't look like they were enjoying being fucked constantly. Some guys did both of them.

"You used to get a kick out of setting up competitions to see who could consume the largest amount of wine. You gave the winner any woman he wanted and watched to see if he could fuck her to completion before passing out." I heard George, and somehow I knew he was telling me the truth.

Another memory emerged. I was cheering on those with big appetites for pleasure and enjoyed watching them make fools of themselves afterward. I think I was the biggest fool of all.

"Uh, Roland, if you don't mind, buddy. I'm not feeling too good. I really need to go."

"If you ask me, Dennis, you really need to stay."

CHAPTER 4

After the meeting, my old drinking buddy, George, and Roland and I went to a restaurant for lunch. I was surprised to find another guy who knew me there. The proprietor. He was a wiry little man with a hyperactive disposition and a French accent. To my delight, he seemed happy to see me and welcomed me with enthusiasm.

I was hoping for more information and maybe even a free lunch. This guy seemed to think I was the coolest.

"Big D, sit here at my best table. I'll bring a nice bottle of wine, and we can talk."

I sensed Roland and George stiffen, so I held up my hand to stop him. "No, thanks. No wine this morning, my friend."

He stared at me while I sat down and got comfortable. "You look different, Big D. Je ne c'est pas que…"

"I feel fine. But I'll let you in on a little secret."

The guy leaned towards me, and I whispered. "I

don't know who you are."

He snapped upright. I quickly added, "Please don't be offended. I don't know who I am either. I have amnesia."

He looked to my companions, and they nodded, confirming it. Once he recovered from his shock, he said, "Mon Deux, now a couple of things make perfect sense. I'm Andre. We have often shared some wine, some laughs, and some women whenever you're in town."

He glanced at my companions, perhaps expecting revulsion. He got none, so he continued. "I saw you Tuesday, but only briefly. You stopped by the restaurant to tell me where the party was. You always arranged the best parties. I arrived there after a late dinner, but you weren't there."

"Yeah, according to witnesses, I fell off the balcony and onto my head. They took me to the hospital and when the x-rays showed that my brains weren't spilling out, they let me go. The ER was pretty busy that night, and I didn't have insurance. At least none that I knew of."

"I'm sorry to hear that. I wish you had called me. I would have been glad to help."

"Do you know anything about me? I mean, my real name? My address?" I was so hopeful. He seemed like a good friend.

"No. I am sorry. We met at a party, and you came to see me here once in a while. I don't know your name except that you're called Big D. The women came up with it. I think it stands for—"

"Yes, that much I know." I was becoming irritated. Why didn't anyone know my real name? Was I living a double life? Did I have a wife and kids somewhere? Geez, I hoped not.

"You know, now that I think about it, there was a guy looking for his brother that night, and the description he gave could have fit you. It didn't occur to me until now."

At last! Some sort of clue. "Really? I have a brother?"

"It might have been your brother. He was steaming mad. He said your father had sent him, and he knew you were around here somewhere."

"I have a father, too?" This was exciting news. Of course, I was hoping that once they knew I broke curfew due to amnesia they would forgive me. "So, how do I find him? Did he leave an address?"

"No, but he did say he'd be back."

"Okay, that's good news." I turned to Roland and said, "Listen, there's something I need to do before I get dragged home by an irate brother."

"What is it?" he asked.

"I need to see a girl. She's working in the warehouse district until four-thirty. Is there any way I can get a ride to the culinary school?" I knew better than to ask for trolley fare.

"I know where it is. I'm sorry. I don't have a car since I lost my license."

George said, "I'd help you out, but I have to get to work, and I take the trolley in the other direction."

Andre shrugged. "I can't leave the place for long, but I should be able to take you over and drop you out front. The parking situation is terrible over there, but if I don't have to stop…"

"No need to stop. If you'll slow down close to the sidewalk, I'll jump out and be grateful."

He laughed and retrieved his coat. Roland stood

when I did and offered me his hand. I clasped it, and he pulled me into a man hug, slapping me on the back a couple of times.

"Take care of yourself. I hope to see you again, but if I don't, just remember that AA works if you work it. In other words, go to as many meetings as possible once you get home."

I nodded and told him I appreciated all he had done for me. And I did. I wasn't an asshole.

Andre stopped in front of the culinary school. As soon as I jogged to the sidewalk, he waved and drove off. I ran up the steps and followed signs to the office. It was only three o'clock, so I might have to wait for her to finish her workday, but that didn't mean I couldn't fuck her in some secluded closet. It had been two days, and I was salivating at the thought of stuffing my full-to-bursting cock inside my willing partner. My penis was diamond hard just picturing her in the doggy position.

I found the office and threw open the door. She had been bending over a low filing cabinet, and her sweet ass was staring me right in the face.

She stood and whirled around. When she saw me, she broke into a wicked grin.

"I've been thinking about you."

I leapt over the desk and swept her into my arms. "I've been thinking about you, too. Where can we go to fuck? I can't wait until you get home."

She giggled and said, "Just close the door. My boss is out for the afternoon, and I'm not expecting anybody."

I leapt over the desk again, closed the door and

pulled off the t-shirt she'd given me. "Let me see your bare ass bent over this desk." My voice was raspy, and her eyes glowed with white-hot sparks. She turned on the radio and did a slow strip for me. I thought I was going to die.

First she unbuttoned her white, silk blouse. Her luscious tits were held prisoner in a white, lace bra. Oh, but it pushed them up high and made her cleavage so succulent. I couldn't complain. Next, she unzipped the back of her black, pencil skirt and let it slide to the floor. She wore a thong and stockings, not pantyhose. She was about to roll down the lace tops, but I was going to lose it if I didn't bury myself in her, soon.

"Leave them on." I breathed heavily as I fumbled with my jeans, struggling out of them as fast as I could.

She giggled and bent over the desk. She spread her legs and pushed her bottom up in the air. My manhood was throbbing. I positioned myself right behind her and shoved my cock in. I was home. Ahhh…

I fucked her hard, and she moaned even harder. I didn't think the radio would drown out her screams when she came, so I pulled out and flipped her over on her back. "When you climax, I'm going to put my mouth over yours, and you can scream into it all you like." I yanked her down over the edge of the desk, so I could bury my shaft inside her again and hold the soft globes of her ass in my hands at the same time.

Oh, God, I loved fucking her where we could get caught. I loved fucking her in private too. Oh, I should just admit it. I loved fucking her. She didn't know it yet, but if I got what I wanted, I'd be fucking her silly for years to come.

She shuddered and her moans were becoming loud, or should I say, louder. I clamped my mouth over hers, and she let go. She convulsed like an epileptic and exhaled a scream into my mouth. Then she took in a deep breath through her nose and did it again as she continued to shake and spasm. It was a good thing I knew how loud this lusty girl could yell and kept my mouth sealed over hers because she kept coming and screaming.

I wondered if all women were capable of this kind of complete and utter abandon to their sexual gratification. She certainly rode hers to the very end. At last, I could let up on her mouth. She gasped and panted but was grinning from ear to ear.

She wrapped her limp legs around me, and I felt the scratch of that stupid anklet. How did she get stockings on if she never removed it? She must take it off sometimes. Why was it so damned important? Another emotion overwhelmed me. It was as uncomfortable as sadness.

Who gave that anklet to her, and why was that person so damn special? Ah, jealousy. That ankle jewelry had to go—along with this new feeling.

"Get those rhinestones out of my back."

She straightened her legs, and I grabbed her by the feet and kept fucking. I glared at the cheap jewelry, and it broke falling to the floor.

"Oh! My anklet!"

"Can't fix it now," I said, as I drove in and out of her at a furious pace. She lay back and panted, gripping the sides of the desk. At last, I came in an earth-shattering orgasm. If she thought I was going to sacrifice my satisfaction she was wrong. She seemed to understand how badly I needed this and didn't try to stop me or complain.

She milked the last drops out of me by clenching my penis with her pussy muscles, hard. When I could breathe again, I asked her a surprising question.

"Ah, Mandy?"

"Yes?" she said, still panting.

"Will you be my girlfriend?"

Sneaking out a little before four, we bounded down the steps holding hands. Out on the sidewalk stood a handsome man. His arms were crossed, and he frowned when he spotted me. I was about to walk right by when he reached out and grabbed my sleeve.

"Where do you think you're going?" he demanded.

What the…? Could this be anklet guy? "Home with my girlfriend. Get your grubby hands off my jacket."

He stood stock-still and looked me up and down but didn't let go of my leather jacket.

"What's your problem, pal?"

He tipped up his chin and stared down his long, straight nose at me. "I'm not your 'pal'."

Some sort of recognition or familiarity occurred. He was right. Whatever we were to each other, we weren't friends. I sensed a long and thorny relationship—something intense and antagonistic. This might be the brother who was searching for me.

"Do I know you?" I asked.

One side of his mouth curled up in a smirk. "Then it's true. You really don't know who you are."

"That's correct. All I know is that some people call me Big D, and another guy thought my name was

Dennis. So what's your vote?"

"Dennis is pretty close. In fact, you've been using that name in English speaking countries for a while."

"Really? So, where am I from, and who the fuck are you?"

"I'm you're half-brother, Apollo. Your name is Dionysus. We live on Mount Olympus."

I gawked at him and couldn't believe the line of bull he was feeding me. He must have thought the fall left me mentally retarded not amnesic.

"Get lost."

"Listen, it was really amusing to see you sitting at AA meetings, and I even enjoyed it when you were mugged and eating out of garbage cans, but after that, we had to step in."

"Who put you up to this?"

"Our father sent me."

"Yeah, sure, and his name is probably Zeus, right?"

"It is."

At that, I burst out laughing. Poor Mandy stood there mute the whole time, but she looked a little nervous. This guy was obviously nuts and making her uncomfortable.

"Come on, Mandy. Let's go home." I put a protective arm around her shoulder. I wouldn't let anything happen to her.

The guy chuckled. "You have a girlfriend. A woman you're living with?"

"What of it?" He was really annoying me now. Why was it so hard to believe I had a girlfriend? I was an attractive man.

"I guess I'll have to be more specific about who you are. You're a god."

"Look, hero worship is nice and all, but…"

He burst out laughing. I was past the point of aggravation and all the way to pissed off.

When he finally stopped laughing he said, "I'm not worshiping your sorry ass. You have cult followers for that, but I'm certainly not one of them. In fact, you're letting them down right now. You're supposed to take over for me in Delphi for the winter months while I vacation in the North. I guess you thought you'd sneak out for the big party, then you fell on your head. Now why doesn't that surprise me?"

Mandy's hand trembled in mine.

Fuming, I yelled, "Just shut up. You're a sick bastard who heard the story of my amnesia and thought you'd play some mind games with me. I don't know who you are, but I know I don't like you. Now get the hell out of here."

I guided Mandy away from him until he called out, "I'm going to tell dad you said that!"

At that point, we just broke into a flat run.

Mandy and I spent the following weeks together. She had to be right about the substitution thing because I never missed drinking when we were having sex. So we had a lot of it. Every morning before she went to work, I'd haul her ass back to bed and screw her doggie style. That was our favorite position. I wanted her to think about me all morning.

Sometimes I'd meet her at work for lunch, and we'd have sex there. The janitor's closet was so small I had to fuck her standing up, but we found a nice position we called the double helix.

If we missed our lunch date, we'd both be horny

as hell. After work, she'd hurry home and I'd attack her the minute she walked in the door, either dragging her to the bedroom or down on the rug. Often, we'd fornicate on the couch.

We named some of our other favorite positions. Let's see, there was the 'on your rocker', the 'hamstring sandwich', the 'Harvey wallbanger', the 'table dance', the 'yoga instructor', the 'tug boat', and the 'jaws of life'.

Once she didn't get a chance to close the door. I grabbed her, lowered her to the kitchen floor and fucked her brains out in the 'greasy spoon' position. The landlady always gave me a wave and a wink after that. She must have spied on us.

Of course, I'm a guy so I'm not emphasizing the love part, but you should know we were absolutely crazy about each other. She enjoyed my sense of humor, even my stupid lack of memory and practical jokes. She said she had laughed more in six weeks with me than she had in her whole life.

I couldn't believe how much she cared about making me happy. She'd bring home edible underwear or whip up a batch of flavored massage oil. Man, could she rub!

My adventurous tiger would try absolutely anything I wanted to do. We made love in public bathrooms, in parking garages, even in the back of the trolley once. She treated me like the man I wanted to be. Hers, forever.

When we had made it through the forty days of Lent with no alcohol, we decided to celebrate with a big party. She and Brenda had repaired their friendship, especially after Mandy told her that I was making her deliriously happy and that I hadn't screwed anyone but her all that time. I also planned to pop the question that night. I had just landed a good job with a party planner and could afford to pull my weight. She was an angel for putting up with my dependency on her for as long as she did.

The damndest thing happened when I went to look at rings though. I knew I couldn't afford any but decided to look anyway—just to torture myself, I guess. I saw the most beautiful diamonds, glittering brightly and just knew Mandy had to have one, if not several. She had never fixed or replaced her anklet. I wanted to give her one with real diamonds to one-up whomever had come before me. I cursed the prices under my breath and had to leave with nothing.

As I walked away from the store, depressed and muttering—wishing like hell I could have found something I could afford, I looked down and lying there right in front of me, I found a brilliant diamond ring on the sidewalk. It was loaded with smaller diamonds surrounding the big one in the center. It reminded me of grabbing her breast and finding her big erect nipple among the smaller stones on her shirt the day I met her.

This ring sparkled more brilliantly than any jewelry in the store. I grabbed it and stuck it in my pocket. I walked a few more paces, and something caught my eye in the gutter. Damned if it wasn't a diamond anklet. Okay, I was no fool. I grabbed that, too.

Our party was scheduled for the following night, and it would be great, but I wanted to surprise her with the anklet first while we were alone. She'd probably wonder if I stole it, but I'd tell her the truth. We always told each other the truth. The only reason I didn't know who had given her the anklet was because of our 'Don't ask, don't tell policy'. Specifically, that meant if we weren't prepared to hear the truth whatever it might be, we shouldn't ask the question.

As soon as I got home, I made dinner. I had been doing the cooking and insisting she eat more than one meal at the school. I prepared a rolled roast with stuffing and cut it into thick pinwheels. I froze a few for later and planned to place her anklet in a pinwheel shape on her empty plate. I'd serve myself first so she could see what we were having, and then I'd serve her diamonds.

She walked through the door, and I threw the roast in the preheated oven a moment before she grabbed my ass. That was all the encouragement I needed.

I practically ripped off her clothes and had her lean over the sink. She teetered, and then stabilized nicely once her forearms were flat against the bottom of the porcelain surface for balance. With her cute ass in the air, she was perfect for banging in the 'bobbing for apples' position. I took a deep breath and appreciated the view as I whipped off my jeans. I was already bare from the waist up, knowing that as soon as she got home all I had to do was yank off my pants, and I'd be fucking her.

I tested her wetness. Oh, yeah. She was moist for me. I positioned my steely cock against her slick folds and penetrated. Once I had her impaled on my penis, I reached around and grabbed her tits, massaging and squeezing them as they hovered over the sink. She was already breathing heavy, and the moaning started as soon as I pinched her hard nipples and rolled them between my fingers.

"Sorry about the total lack of foreplay, darling, but I'll make up for that later."

"Don't apologize. Feels good," she breathed.

I knew she loved a good reach-around so I found her clit and rubbed. Her moans sounded like a wolf in heat.

"That's it, baby. I'm going to play with your clit until you have as many orgasms as you can before the roast is done."

"I want to," she squeaked. "But the sink might not stay comfortable for lengthy lovemaking."

"Fucking, honey. Say 'fucking.' It feels good to say it and makes us both hot as hell."

She giggled.

I could see I was going to have to help out this sweet southern girl. "I'm fucking you. We're fucking. Say it."

"You say it!"

She was the perfect woman. A lady in public and my own personal, hot, horny honey in private. But she still had a hard time with the dirty talk.

"I'll conjugate it," I said. "I fuck, you fuck, we fuck, they fuck. I fucked, you fucked, we fucked, they fucked—"

"We all got fucked!" she cried out.

Sure enough, she shook with each spasm then let out her signature screams alternating with hardy giggles.

As soon as she had taken a few gasps of breath, I held on tight and picked her up, still speared on my cock. I moved her to the kitchen table and fucked her some more. I was starting to feel my own climax building. "I wish I could hold off until you've had a dozen orgasms, but that isn't going to happen, babe."

"That's okay. I probably wouldn't live through it."

"We'll come together," I said. I found her nub and teased it until we were both on the verge. She started her long, lusty scream, and as her pussy clenched, delightful vibrations wracked my body. I jerked and grunted and crashed over the edge with her.

When I finally pulled out, I collapsed on the linoleum. She moved as if melting off the table onto the floor beside me. We both panted for a while before she spoke.

"Okay, I said something for you. Now, will you say something for me?"

"Sure, what is it?"

"I love you."

CHAPTER 5

Getting up, I reached for my jeans and bought a moment to think. Of course, I loved her, and I'm sure I would have said it at some point, but, damn… Wouldn't it be more effective if I said it on my own and not because I was asked to? While I was hopping into my jeans, I stole a glance at her face. Not good. She was beginning to frown and a faint shimmer of tears seemed to be forming.

"Baby, don't do that." I reached over and put a finger under her chin. She tried to hide behind closed eyes, but a tear leaked out of the corner. "Hey, come on, now. You wouldn't want me to say it just because you asked me to, right?" At which point, she burst into tears.

I had never seen her cry like that. She sounded heartbroken. What did I say?

"What is it, babe? What's making you cry?"

"You," she yelled and ran into the bedroom, slamming the door behind her.

Now I knew why men don't understand women. I

thought Mandy must be different. We had never had any misunderstandings at all. Was it that time of the month?

Wait a minute! She hadn't had a… Uh oh.

I ran to the bedroom door and stopped myself a second before I barged in. Be sensitive, I told myself and knocked.

"Mandy, honey? Can I come in?"

"No!"

I stood there, mute, wondering what to do next. I knocked again. "Please, baby—um, I mean, honey. Darling! We need to talk."

A few moments later, she opened the bedroom door, her beautiful body hidden under a robe. I reached for her, and she recoiled. She walked around the bed and plopped down on it, facing away from me.

"Don't be ashamed, Mandy. This kind of thing happens."

She sniffed. "Well, it's never happened to me before."

Dear Zeus. My heart was aching just witnessing her pain. Time for some serious bling. I still had the anklet in my pocket and extracted it. Walking around to the other side of the bed, I kneeled in front of her and took her hand. She offered no resistance. I turned her hand, palm up and kissed it. Then I lay the diamonds in a spiral right where my lips had been.

She burst into tears again. What the hell was I doing wrong?

A loud sound, as if someone was clearing his throat, startled me.

That nut-bag who had called himself Apollo appeared in the doorway and leaned against the door jam.

"Looks like you've really gone and done it now, little brother."

"What the fuck are you doing here? How did you get in?"

"I'm a god, remember? I'm here to bail out your ass and take you home."

I shot to my feet and even though I was shaking inside, I was prepared to fight off this insane stalker if I had to.

"Look, I don't know what your damage is, but you need to leave before I call the cops."

"You're the one with the damage, little brother." He stood erect with a wide stance, his hands on his hips. "You don't even remember being a god. I thought it might be amusing to watch you struggle along as a mortal for a while, but you've ceased to entertain our father."

Mandy grabbed my arm. Her eyes widened in terror.

"Do something, Dennis!"

I was furious. No one was going to threaten my future wife and child. "Look, buddy. I've had enough of you. Get out of my way before I go right through you."

He didn't budge.

I charged him and as I did, I felt my body stretch and become so heavy I dropped on my hands and knees. Mandy screamed.

It didn't matter. I was going to get this guy out of our apartment regardless of how my body was reacting. Suddenly, I felt a surge of power. I looked down at what I thought were my hands, and they had turned to hooves. I lowered my head and thought I saw horns. So much the better. I chased my half-brother out the door and stopped on the porch. The boards creaked underneath me. I turned enough to see Mandy's horrified expression as she peeked around the corner. Then the porch gave way.

"Where the hell am I?"

Apollo folded his arms and smirked. "You don't recognize it?"

I glanced all around me. I was in a round room with rock walls. My asshole brother stood in the only opening.

Inside the room was a large bed with white linens and a lot of white curtains blowing in an invisible breeze. No chairs, no tables. Nothing but a bed. Ordinarily, that would be enough for me to entertain friends, but something wasn't right.

"No. I don't recognize it. Where are we and why?"

"You're in the time-out room on Mount Olympus."

"The what?"

"That's right. You weren't raised here. Well, if you had been, you probably wouldn't need this place at your age. Instead you were spoiled by Nymphs."

"So, what are you telling me? When the rest of you were 'bad' you'd have to sit here and think about what you did?"

"You got it."

"Why are we here? Are you the boss of me now?"

"Of course not. This is where dad told me to take you. Both of you cretins who taunted Pele will be getting your own worst version of punishment. Yours, my extroverted little brother, is total isolation for one year."

I was speechless. I couldn't believe what I was hearing. Then I realized he couldn't hold me there. I was a friggin' god, if he was telling me the truth. So I laughed and attempted to push past him to walk out.

Next thing I knew, I was blown backward and landed on the bed. "What the?"

And my stupid brother was laughing his ass off.

When he could speak, he said, "It wouldn't be much of a punishment if you could just walk right out of here, would it?"

"What was that? Some kind of force field?"

"Yup."

"Can you get out?"

"Yup."

"Then, get out!"

Gloating, he shrugged one shoulder. "I will. And a year from now, I'll come back. By then you'll be so glad to see anyone, you'll probably be a whole lot nicer to me."

"Don't count on it," I growled.

"Okay."

He turned to leave, but then it occurred to me that no one had seen to my basic needs.

"Wait. What about food, water and a bathroom? Am I supposed to sit in my own filth until I starve to death?"

He laughed. "You don't get it, do you?"

"Get what?"

"You're a god, stupid. And apparently you're a stupid god. You don't need to eat, drink or go to the bathroom unless you want to."

"And what if I want to?"

He grinned. "Then you're shit out of luck little

brother, because no one—and I mean no one is allowed to see you or talk to you until the year is up."

A deep shuddering dread permeated my soul. Suddenly my punishment was making sense. I was to be all alone with nothing to do to. No one else to focus on. Just me and my brain for an entire year.

Suddenly my thoughts returned to Mandy. Oh, no. What must she be thinking? She watched as I turned into a giant bull, broke through her porch and disappeared before hitting the ground.

"You have to tell Mandy what happened."

"Uh, no I don't."

"Yes, you do! Even you can't be that much of a shithead."

"Sorry. Just following orders."

He wasn't sorry at all. I had to appeal to his sense of fairness. "She's innocent in all of this. If you don't tell her what happened, she's apt to think she's lost her mind. That's not right."

"You should have thought about that before," Apollo said.

"Before what? Before knowing I was a friggin' god and could turn myself into just about any shape I wanted at any moment? Before you came for me, claiming to be my older, better brother?"

He studied his fingernails. "Well…"

"Please. Go to her and explain."

"Sorry. No can do. All I can do is convey your concerns to dad and whatever he decides goes."

"But how will I know what he says?"

"You won't."

Now I was pissed. I mean, I was angry before, but now I was really friggin' mad.

And that's when he disappeared.

A year later, still on Mount Olympus, I was taken to my father, who was sitting on his throne. Since my memory had been restored I knew who I was—Dionysus, god of wine, women and party. And, more importantly, I knew who he was—Zeus, the all-powerful ruler of the world. I had to tread carefully, but he couldn't put me off any longer. I had served my punishment and this conversation had to happen.

I sat at his feet and proceeded to explain myself. I had a year to think up excuses and ways in which to absolve myself of all wrong doing, but I'd also had enough time to realize none of that would work anymore.

I had to be honest and I was. I recounted everything that happened with Pele. I expressed my real remorse about leaving my best friend, Epi—my partner in crime—to face his punishment without me. I confessed that I escaped to New Orleans, because I wanted to buy some time for Epimetheus to get away. I figured Zeus would go after me, knowing I was always the instigator. Oh, and I remembered Mardi Gras was coming. Hiding in that crowd seemed like a good way to disappear and have some fun at the same time.

I told him about my fall off the balcony and about Mandy and Brenda taking me home. I gave him all the details of my time living as a human with amnesia, and not once did he laugh at me. Then I asked if I could go 'home' to my human family.

He raised his eyebrows and stared at me for a long time. At last he spoke. "After all you went through as a human, you would choose to return to that life? Is there something you aren't telling me? Do you have a harem waiting? It's not like you to be happy with the mundane, son."

"I've told you the entire story and, yes, I still want to return to my life in New Orleans. I want to marry Mandy and raise our children. I want to make a good life for them either here, or there, it doesn't matter to me. It only matters that we're together."

Zeus would probably try to talk me out of it. I had to remain firm and refuse to let him sway me.

"You know she's mortal, as your mother was. She will age and die as your mother would have if I hadn't accidentally incinerated her. Oh, I could kick myself for that. The point is, you will not die, even if you want to."

"Yes, I know that. I'll love her until the day she passes and beyond, if only you'll let me. I'd rather anticipate and expect that painful event than go through eternity without ever knowing true love."

Zeus scratched his mighty head. "I don't understand you, boy. You've gotten yourself into plenty of scrapes, and I've had to bail you out a number of times, but this is the first time you ever wanted to take responsibility for your actions. I'm puzzled by the change in you, yet I have to admit, I'm moved."

"I've always been in plenty of trouble, father, that's true. I've caused a great deal of it and I'm not proud of myself—yet. I want to be. I want to do the right thing."

"You sound like Apollo."

"Fuck Apollo. He was the one who ripped me away from her and brought me here against my will. She doesn't even know how much I love her. She doesn't know that I know about our son. I want to take her in my arms and say 'I love you' over and over and show her how much I mean it and how well I can provide for our family. Father, I would die for her—if I could." I was absolutely serious.

Zeus took a deep breath and nodded. "Ordinarily, I would have thought that Apollo had finally had an influence on you, but I know he had nothing to do with it. Apparently, the change has been brought about by true love. I swear I never thought I'd see the day. If this Mandy is really as special as that, then marry her and raise a ton of kids. If you want to waste your time on that crap, be my guest. I give you my blessing."

I jumped in the air and whooped. Finally! He was going to let me go to her at last. As I danced, grapevines grew all over the mountain.

As I was dancing out of Zeus's throne room, guess who I bumped into? My old buddy Epimetheus. We clasped forearms, but he didn't let go when I did.

"What gives?" I asked.

"I thought I might have to hold onto you, so you don't take off in the middle of a conversation."

Oh. That. Well, I guess I had it coming. "Look, I'm sorry. I really thought Zeus would follow me and you'd have the sense to disappear."

He rolled his eyes.

"Whatever he did to you, I imagine it was just as awful as what I went through. Maybe worse. Is there any way I can make it up to you?"

He smirked. "Yeah, actually. There is."

Uh-oh. I didn't like that look, but I owed him.

"Lay it on me. What can I do?"

"There's an old boss of mine that I'd like you to turn into a male praying mantis."

I reared back and laughed my head off. Considering the fact that some female praying mantis would probably fuck him and then bite his head off, I was sure the bastard must have had it coming. "It sure sounds like he was after a special piece of tail and you need some satisfaction."

"He wanted Pandora."

My eyes almost bugged out of my head. Was my poor brother delusional? Now he was talking to his dead wife? What the hell had Zeus done to him?

"I know what you're thinking," he said.

"You do?"

"Yeah. You think I've lost my marbles because Pandora died many years ago."

I nodded, trying to look as nonjudgmental as I could. After all, the poor guy had probably been laughed at plenty.

"She's alive. Reincarnated. In the middle of my job from hell, we found each other again."

I winced. "That's what Zeus did to you? He made you get a—a *job?*"

"Yeah, but like I said…it was worth it. At first Pandy didn't know who she was, but I finally managed to remind her—if you know what I mean." He elbowed me and winked.

"Ah, I get it. Good for you! So, I take it this boss was a real shithead."

"You know it."

"Did he try to force himself on her?"

"No, but only because she tried to kick a hole through his testicles."

I nodded in understanding. "I figured the punishment must fit the crime."

The evil grin he gave me told me all I needed to know. "Okay, if you take me to this asshat right now and I let you watch, will we be square?"

He chuckled. "I don't know how square we'll ever be, but at least we'll be even."

And off we went.

I finally had permission to see Mandy, and I couldn't wait. I only hoped I could convince her to see me. After what had happened between us the last time I was with her, I wasn't exactly sure she'd want to. She probably thought I had used her and taken off just like most gods do.

She might not even realize I'm a god. She may have thought Apollo was the one to change me into a bull. I'd just have to prove it to her, and I knew exactly how I wanted to do that.

Over the past year, I had replayed every moment of our short time together. I realized we'd had enormous passion and fun, yet I'd never held her tenderly, looked deeply into her eyes and said the words she deserved to hear. "I love you." If I'd had any doubts, they were long gone. My father did his best to make me forget her, but I couldn't. Every time I closed my eyes, I'd see her beautiful smile and sparkling blue eyes, her cute freckled nose and her long, red hair all mussed from making love. I'd hear her laughter in my dreams and wake up reaching for her. No other goddess, nymph or mortal held any interest for me. Yup, I was gob-smacked in love all right.

When I'd arrived back on Mount Olympus, I'd punched my brother Apollo and told him never to speak to me again. Of course, that didn't last. But when he did speak, he came with news that made me unspeakably happy. I was a father. My beautiful Mandy and our son were both healthy and doing well. Now I was going to see them, at last.

It broke my heart to think about Mandy struggling as a single parent, trying to make ends meet. I couldn't wait to shower her with all the luxuries she could ever want. A mansion and staff to care for it, a loving nanny—maybe one of the nymphs who raised me. After all they did a great job, right? And, of course, my undivided attention and all the great sex she could handle.

Mandy's house was empty, and I began to panic. Then I remembered someone I could see who would know what happened to her. I dreaded the confrontation as I arrived at her apartment in the French Quarter.

"You!" Brenda blocked her doorway, arms crossed and legs apart. I don't think she wanted to let me in.

"Please. Brenda, I have to find Mandy. I came as soon as I could. I mean that."

"Yeah, right."

"I did. Look, I know who I am now, and I can help. Just please tell me where my girlfriend and son are. I'll help you, too."

"We're not interested in your 'help'."

"Brenda? Is someone at the door? Did you say you need help?"

I recognized the voice immediately. It was like the

most beautiful melody to meet my ears since Pan played his flute.

"No, hon. I've got it."

"Please, Brenda," I implored with my eyes as well as my voice. I didn't want to just brush by her even though I easily could have.

She rolled her eyes and said, "Come in. They're in the bedroom."

"Thank you. I promise you won't be sorry."

I paused at the bedroom door and watched her for a few seconds. She was more beautiful than ever. She had cut her long curls into soft, shoulder-length, auburn waves. Her eyes sparkled in the candlelight as she sang to our son, gently rocking him to sleep. What a wonderful mother she was. I'd be proud to call her the mother of all my offspring.

I wouldn't run away from feelings. Not this time. I was a little peeved at Zeus for making me wait a year to decide what I really wanted, especially when I knew all along.

Okay, she was laying him in his crib and my baby boy was sleeping peacefully. This would be the perfect time. "Mandy?"

She lifted her head and froze, her mouth open in shock. I pulled out the ring I had 'found'. Now I understood that every strong wish I had made during my amnesia had come true because I was a friggin' god the whole time. I held the ring out to her so she could see I was serious.

She moved slowly, as if in a daze, but she arrived at the door. "May I help you?"

"Oh, no. Don't tell you have amnesia, too!"

She snorted. "I should be so lucky."

"I have to talk to you. Please. It's very important."

She bit her lower lip and hesitated, then nodded and stepped aside.

I motioned her to sit on the bed. The one we made love on for the first time. She sat and I went down on one knee in front of her.

"Mandy. I love you. I've loved you from the day we met, and I'll love you until the day you die. No. Longer than that. I'll probably love you forever because I'm immortal, but that's beside the point.

"The point is I was taken to Mount Olympus against my will. I was forced to think about my behavior for a year, wishing the whole time I could just get back to you. I didn't realize that night you were taking my words the wrong way. I wanted to say everything in my heart, and I messed it up."

She smiled and pulled up the hem of her slacks. "I know," she said. Her diamond anklet sparkled in the candlelight.

This was it. The right moment had arrived. I presented the ring to her again and asked her to marry me. She smiled slowly, but shook her head no.

"No? You're saying 'no'?"

"Yes, I'm saying 'no'. You need to prove yourself, Dennis."

"Dionysus."

"Whatever…"

"So be it." I waved my arm and sent a cascade of diamonds raining from the ceiling. I gathered them and set them at her feet.

She seemed startled at first but blinked and said, "No, you have to do more than that."

Okay. Knowing how much she liked to wear her bling, I waved my arm in a bigger arc and brought down necklaces, tiaras, rings, bracelets, anklets and brooches in every style and size. I caught as many of them as I could and presented her with an armful spilling over. I could see her eyes widen as she stared at the pile of treasure.

"Yeah, that's all very nice, Dionysus, but I need you to prove yourself in other ways."

Geez, she was tough to win over. But I would! "Anything, my sweet. What would you like?"

She straightened her posture and narrowed her eyes. "Well, for one thing, I need a promise and some kind of painful consequence if you break it."

"I'll be pained plenty if I ever hurt you again, especially with a broken promise. But if it helps, you can give me one hard kick in the nuts without repercussions."

She giggled.

I piled the jewels in her lap, and to protect my own, I sat beside her. "Okay, lay it on me, sweetheart. What do you want from me?"

She took a deep breath. Uh oh, it must be a long list.

"I want you to provide a good example for our son to follow. I've read up on you, and I know you're the biggest bad boy on Mount Olympus. What I need you to do, specifically, is to give up all orgies and three-ways until and unless I choose to participate."

"Done."

"There's more."

"I was afraid of that."

One side of her sexy mouth curled into a smile. "Next, I want you to live here, in New Orleans, with me and our son, Brendon, and never leave us again."

"Done. Mandy, I won't leave you. Either of you. I don't think you know how much I love you, but I'll show you every day and every night." I winked, but she didn't seem impressed.

"And no supernatural stuff around the kids," she continued. "They're going to find out, but I don't want them to be scared to death like I was."

"Done. Unless you want it, of course. I could ask Zeus to make you immortal so we can be together, always."

"He can do that?"

"Of course he can. He's the friggin' god of everything."

"Let me think about that for a while." She tipped her head and looked up as if mulling it over.

"I don't want to lose you," I whispered.

"Can you behave yourself forever? I know that's asking a lot."

"I can. I will. For you, I'll do anything."

She smiled. "Okay then. I'm yours. Oh, but there are a couple more things…"

I rolled my eyes. "What else?"

"I want you to get a job."

"I'll get a job working construction. I can help the city."

"Good. And I don't want any Olympians knowing where we are. At least until the kids are grown. I don't want them popping in and out."

"Not even Epi and Pandy? But they're my best friends."

"If they can keep your location a secret, I guess it's okay, but I *especially* don't want anyone telling your rotten stepmother, Hera, where to find you."

"She hates me, you know."

"I know." Mandy placed her hand on my thigh. "Can you blame her? Zeus cheated on her with your mom, Semele. I mean, she was just a dumb princess who didn't know any better, but he sure did. Hera can't exactly take it out on him, and your mom had already burned to ashes by the time she found out, so you're all she had left to torture. It seems Hera's got a real nasty, jealous streak."

"Yeah, then she made everyone who tried to protect me either go crazy or die. If it weren't for my dad, I wouldn't be here now."

I stood up and started pacing, all the vicious crap she pulled came flooding back to me. "Did you know that he had to change me into a goat and hide me on Mount Nysa to be raised by nymphs? If he hadn't done that, she'd have killed me when I was just a child."

Mandy crossed her arms and leaned back against the pillows. She was still covered in brilliant, sparkling bling. "Uh huh, which leads me to believe that nymphs shouldn't be raising children, especially not omnipotent ones. Look at your reputation! You're going to have to go a ways to convince your son that you're only using your power for good. I don't want him raised by one of those 'Do what I say, not what I do' fathers. I can't stand that. You should keep going to AA on occasion. That'll help you keep things in perspective."

"Okay, okay! This is more than one promise, you know. Is there anything else?"

"One more thing."

"Dear Zeus, what is it?" She was relentless! I must have seriously compromised her trust. This beautiful woman who gave her trust to me so innocently only a year ago couldn't do that now, and it wasn't even my fault. "Tell me. I'll give you anything. Do anything.

Name it."

"Get rid of this crap that's all over me." She pointed to the diamonds and jewelry covering her lap.

I couldn't believe what I was hearing. "I thought you liked a little bling?"

"Yeah, a little. I don't need all of this."

I started by sending back the tiaras then hesitated. "How much do you need?"

"Just the anklet."

"But…"

"And the ring." Her smile grew and she extended her left hand.

I placed it on her finger. She grinned, and we hugged, overjoyed. With a sweep of my hand all the other jewelry disappeared, and she jumped into my arms.

"I knew you loved me," she said. "I knew the minute you gave me the anklet. You hated the other one, yet you replaced it because you knew how much it meant to me."

I nuzzled her neck and realized that I still didn't know who had given her the other one. Now that she was wearing my ring, the answer didn't really matter.

"So why was the other one so special?"

"My mother gave it to me. My dad had given it to her when they were dating. She said he gave it to her the night he first told her he loved her. It was just rhinestones, but I always loved looking at it when I was a kid. She gave it to me when he gave her one made with real diamonds."

"Like the one I gave you."

Her mouth dropped open, and she stared at her ankle. "I thought they looked awfully real. I just thought they were making better fake jewelry these days. How did you pay for it?"

"I didn't. I found it in the gutter."

She laughed. "Exactly where I found you!"

"Yup. I'm a diamond in the rough but I'll clean up real nice, sweetheart. I promise. You'll see."

ABOUT THE AUTHOR

Ashlyn Chase describes herself as an Almond Joy bar. A little nutty, a little flaky, but basically sweet, wanting only to give her fans a satisfying, reading experience.

She worked as a psychiatric nurse for several years and spent a few more years working for the Red Cross. She credits her sense of humor to her former careers since comedy helped preserve whatever was left of her sanity. Ashlyn holds a degree in behavioral sciences and has been trained as a fine artist, registered nurse, hypnotherapist, and interior designer.

Most writers, whether they're aware of it or not, have a 'theme'…some sort of thread that runs through all of their books, uniting the whole mishmash into an identifiable signature. Ashlyn's identified theme involves characters who reinvent themselves. It's no wonder since she has reinvented herself numerous times. Finally content with her life, she lives in beautiful New Hampshire with her true-life hero husband and they're owned by a spoiled brat cat.

Email: ash@ashlynchase.com
List of Ashlyn's other published books:
Tug of Attraction, Lachesis Publishing 9/28/2015
The Cupcake Coven, Lachesis Publishing 6/22/2015
Kissing with Fangs, Sourcebooks 3/4/14
How to Date a Dragon, Sourcebooks 9/3/13
Flirting Under a Full Moon, Sourcebooks 4/2/13
Immortally Yours, Ellora's Cave 1/13/12

The Vampire Next Door, Sourcebooks 8/1/2011
The Werewolf Upstairs, Sourcebooks: 2/1/2011
Strokes, (with Dalton Diaz) Ellora's Cave: 8/3/2010
Strange Neighbors, Sourcebooks: 6/1/10
Dear Sexy Lexie, Ellora's Cave: 3/17/10
Green Card, Total-e-Bound: 12/14/2009
Love Cuffs, (with Dalton Diaz) Ellora's Cave:
9/28/2008
Death by Delilah, Ellora's Cave: 4/11/2008
Quivering Thighs, Ellora's Cave: 2/8/2008
Demolishing Mr. Perfect, Ellora's Cave: 8/15/2007
Wonder Witch, Ellora's Cave: 6/15/2007
Being Randy, Ellora's Cave: May 2, 2007
Heaving Bosoms, Cerridwen Press: (Now Blush)
3/15/2007
Vampire Vintage, Ellora's Cave: 3/14/2007
Buy links can be found on my website.
http://www.ashlynchase.com

Ashlyn communicates with fans regularly on her
own yahoo loop, through blogs, and via social media.
Sign up for her newsletter on her website. That
number again is, http://www.ashlynchase.com Don't
worry. No spam. Newsletters only go out when
there's a new release to announce.

http://groups.yahoo.com/group/ashlynsnewbestfrie
nds/
http://www.twitter.com/GoddessAsh
http://www.facebook.com/authorashlynchase/
http://ashlynchase.blogspot.com/ (For monthly
news re: guest blogs, book signings, etc.)
http://casablancaauthors.blogspot.com/ Monthly
contributor

Made in the USA
Las Vegas, NV
12 March 2022

45547653R00105